RACE AGAINST TIME

SANDS OF TIME TRILOGY - BOOK 2

C.J. PETERSON

ISBN - 978-1-952041-42-6 (paperback)

ISBN - 978-1-952041-43-3 (ebook)

This book is dedicated to my loving husband and dear family who love and support me. You all mean more to me than you will ever know. Thank you! I love you!

This trilogy is also dedicated to my mom, **Sue Mann**. *We lost her in January 2021. She never hesitated to take other kids under her wing to guide, direct, and pray for them. She was a prayer warrior and an encourager until the end! Her legacy of praying the family through all our good times and bad will never be forgotten. I only hope to continue to grow in my prayer life to be as strong as she was! Mom, you are loved and missed, but we all know you're up in Heaven making sure to keep an eye on all of us!*

A portion of the proceeds from this series go to:
www.daretodream-dallas.org

Their mission: *To pick up the broken pieces of the lives of wounded youngsters in group homes, shelters, detention centers, and orphanages by providing life-skills education and ministry through role model speakers, cultural experiences (art, music, and dance), and one-on-one mentoring.* **Who they serve:** *Youth between the ages of ten and eighteen, living in shelters, foster homes, group homes, detention centers and orphanages. Many have been abused and neglected and do not have a father present in their lives. Partnerships have been developed with Juvenile*

Departments, State Youth Commissions, youth shelters, group homes and orphanages.

To learn more about C.J. Peterson, you can find her online at:
http://cjpetersonwrites.com/
'While the stories are fiction, the journey is real!'

CONTENTS

SUMMARY

Professor Noah Roth is possessive of *his children* – the children he created by genetic manipulation. When Ben and Hope took Holly and Blake in order to give them a better life, they knew their days were numbered. Continuously looking over their shoulders, they still missed it when the Clinic made their move by sending a group, along with two gifted after them.

Adam and Deanna Roth thought they were on the right side of things, until they ran into the other two gifted – Holly and Blake. Presented with another perspective, Deanna and Adam agree to help Holly, Blake, and Sheriff Wyatt rescue Hope and Ben, as long as they help Deanna and Adam rescue the other siblings still under the control of Professor Roth.

As the five head toward Maine, the youth group kids who became close to Blake and Holly over the last few weeks, decided to help them by doing research. Unbeknownst to them, they stumbled onto information the Clinic did not want out. After each of their homes were invaded, the kids had to make a choice – join the others in the rescue attempt, or stay home, therefore putting their families in danger. Will they make it in time to help the others, or will they be too late? It's a *Race Against Time*!

Joshua 1:9 – "Have I not commanded you? Be strong and courageous. Do not be frightened, and do not be dismayed, for the Lord your God is with you wherever you go."

"Time slips through our hands like grains of sand never to return again. Those who use time wisely are rewarded with rich, productive and satisfying lives." Robin Sharma

Characters In The Sands Of Time Trilogy & Series:

Holly   Blake   Deanna   Adam

Charlie   Eddie   Freya   Gemma   Isabelle

The Gifted Maine Teens

Shawn   Mac   Colby

Lindsey   Megan   Tanya

Willow Bend Teens

MAKING GOOD TIME

"Like as the waves make toward the pebbled shore, so do our minutes hasten to their end." William Shakespeare

*H*ope opened her eyes. To her horror, she instantly recognized the room as one of the isolation rooms at the Maine campus. On her breaks those many years before she left, she would explore the compound. During one of her ventures, she discovered a floor with five metal doors on either side. A nauseating cacophony of vomit, urine, and other bodily fluids, mixed with bleach made Hope cringe. The pungent odor overwhelmed her senses. It carried the stench of death and terror. In its day, this old building was used for nefarious purposes.

Room was a kind word to describe the space. There were no windows. The walls were steel, and the floor was concrete. There was a commode in the corner with a small sink next to it. Other than the prison-like amenities, the six-by-six-foot room was bare. The walls and floor were painted orange, but you could barely see the faded color through the rust corroding the metal. A single light hung from wires, creating a short, making the bulb blink.

As if being in the cell was not bad enough, zip ties secured Hope's ankles and wrists to a rusty metal chair. She had no idea how long she had been there, nor what happened to Ben, Wyatt, or the kids. All she knew was someone would come twice a day. They would cut the zip ties so she could eat, let her go to the bathroom, and then secure her once more.

The unmistakable *click* of the door closing at the end of the hall made her jerk her head to look. Faint voices closed in on her. Not just one set of shoes. There was a team coming this time.

Ch'click!

The door creaked open slowly, presenting Professor Noah Roth himself, along with three other men.

"Good evening, Hope…or should I say, Grace?" Professor Roth said with a sly smile. His strong English accent bled through every syllable. She used to adore his accent – before she knew the monster behind the voice. As a matter of fact, many of the women admired him on the compound. His bold features, dark-brown eyes, black hair, and firm frame attracted them at first, but his brilliance and charisma endeared them to him. Not until they were firmly entrenched within the system, did they discover the madness behind the man, and then fear took over.

Hope sat frozen, refusing to acknowledge the man–beast.

"No snarky come back? My people have shared stories of your wit. They said you were very amusing. However, they also said you only care about one question: *What happened to Ben*?" When she still did not respond, he slowly circled her chair. "Ben. The one who you fled this facility with, along with two of my children."

"Killing their mothers doesn't make them your children."

"Wrong!" he shouted, making her jump. Resting his hands on

his knees in front of her, he leaned so he was eye-level with her, and insisted, "Their mothers died during childbirth. I have the records. They died of natural causes."

"Natural causes do not cause someone to bleed out of their eyes, nose, mouth, and ears. They also did not all die in child-birth. I know for a fact the two we left behind had a mother when we left. You killed them."

He stood, throwing his hands dramatically in the air. "Why in the world would I do that? I would never take a child from its mother. I have compassion for all the little ones, and I've raised them out of the kindness of my heart. These children were raised in this magnificent facility, with the stunning forest landscapes surrounding us."

"You are a real piece of work!" Hope shot back. "You killed their mothers, so you would have full custody of those kids. You did it, so you could do whatever you wanted to them! And you might want to take a look around your castle, your highness. It's in serious disrepair."

"I made each of those children stronger."

"You treated them like lab rats!" Hope's heart broke at the thought. "I promise you they were not raised with love like Blake and Holly!"

"Where are my two little darlings?"

Hope narrowed her eyes. "They will never be yours."

"Oh yes, they will. I sent two of my strongest to ensure their safe return."

"Then why aren't they here?" Hope challenged. "I've been here for almost two weeks. Yet, you're still asking where they are. That tells me you have no idea where any of them are right now. If you did, you wouldn't need me."

"You are correct," he said as he resumed his slow circle of the chair. "I will use you as the bait to lure them back here. It will not take long. My spies tell me Deanna and Adam will awaken soon. I have yet to ascertain the plan after that. Rest assured, I will find out."

"When they get here, they'll take you out themselves."

"No, they won't. You're alive to assure their compliance. You see, I want them to watch you die in front of their very eyes. I want them to understand what happens to those who come against me and mine."

Hope gulped as she gripped the chair to keep herself under control. She did not want to give him the satisfaction of knowing he got to her.

"You will only live as long as you are of value to me. No one takes anything from me and lives to talk about it." Turning to one of the men, he ordered, "Give her the first dose." With that, he left into the hall.

Hope's body trembled as she eyed the liquid already loaded into the syringe one of the nurses held. "What is that?"

The nurse sneered, as he took the cover off the needle. "We'll just call it your daily medication."

"No!" Hope shouted, struggling in her seat. "What is that? Tell me!"

Two men flanked either side of Hope to hold her down. The third lifted her shirt sleeve and jammed the needle into her arm. Fear and panic took over. Trembling, she watched while the amber liquid emptied into her arm. This caused her heart to race, sending the vile liquid through her system at an alarming rate.

When the warmth permeated her body, her vision blurred. Feeling her head swimming, she desperately fought to find one thing to focus on...*anything*.

"That won't take long," the man who injected her announced. "Now for the other one," he said as he pulled another pre-filled syringe from his pocket, and they headed out the door.

When the door closed, Hope heard the door lock click, sealing her in once again. At the rate she was going, it would be her tomb.

"He doesn't have much left in him. Doesn't Professor Roth still want him alive when they get here?" asked one of the nurses.

"We follow his orders," insisted another nurse.

Hope heard another lock sound. Then, she heard the unmistakable string of vulgar words emit from a man she had come to love as a brother over the years – *Ben!*

◁◁◁◁◁◁

"HOW ARE we going to do this?" Holly asked from her position in the third row. Wyatt bought a dark-blue, fifteen-passenger van for the trip. He considered renting one, but decided if they were bringing back the other kids, they would need a bigger van anyway. Blake sat in the front passenger seat while Wyatt drove. Holly's decision to sit in the third row was so she could keep an eye on Deanna and Adam, who claimed the second bench seat.

"I believe we'll have to take this one day at a time," Wyatt said, merging onto the highway. "We need to learn to trust each other."

"That's easier said than done," Adam mumbled.

Blake turned and frowned at Adam. "Just because I can't read your mind doesn't mean I can't hear you. Trust in this situation is something we're all going to have to learn. You and Deanna are our brother and sister. As family, we will not stop until all of our family is out from under Professor Roth, whether you believe it or not."

"From this point forward, we will not intentionally harm you," Holly added. "Our lives depend on each other."

Deanna sighed as she looked out the window from her seat behind Wyatt. She decided to memorize what the outside world looked like in case this went sideways and she was once again sequestered to the compound in Maine.

"Whatever you think you know, I promise you we are

nothing like what Professor Roth told you," Blake continued. "We were raised in a different environment. Just like you want to get our other brothers and sisters out, we want to get the others out, as well as Hope and Ben. We're all in this together. Professor Roth knows we can effectively take each other out. That's why he sent you. Imagine his face when we show up together."

Deanna chuckled under her hand. She was certain the look would be priceless! *Working with these two may not be so bad after all.* Her only questions were *Would they fulfill their promise and help the other sets once Hope and Ben were rescued? And what would it cost them to get everyone out?* They already lost Charlie. She did not want to lose anyone else. "All right," Deanna finally said.

"What?" Adam asked.

"We'll do this. It'll be worth it just to see him fail."

"He's our dad!" Adam objected.

"Are you really going to tell me you love that man?" Deanna challenged.

"I-no," Adam admitted, looking down. "He's our dad, though."

"He's a sperm donor," Wyatt interjected. "A dad looks after and cares for his children. A dad teaches them right and wrong in a loving way. A dad is there to make sure his children are safe, secure, and well cared for. Professor Roth killed your mothers. Professor Roth pushed your brother to the point of death. Professor Roth shoved you into isolation rooms when you didn't do what he wanted, or beat you or your closest sibling if you didn't obey. Professor Roth is not a dad, nor a father. He is a dictator and a monster."

"You seem passionate about this," Deanna pointed out.

"You were raised in a horrific environment," Wyatt said, staying focused on the road ahead while periodically glancing at the GPS. "You should have been raised in love. I've seen both sides of this working in law enforcement. There's one thing that really sets me off. That's when children are mistreated. I've been around and helped raise these two since they were a year old. I wish I could have helped raise all of you. Can you imagine, with the visions Blake showed you, how much different life would be for you if you were raised by Ben and Hope?"

Adam considered Wyatt's words. "For one thing, Charlie would still be alive," he said.

"You guys would have friends and learned to have fun. Who knows? You may also have a girlfriend or boyfriend," Holly added.

"That's not to mention –"

"We get it. Trust me," Deanna cut Blake off. "No reason to dwell on what never was." She turned her attention back to the passing countryside.

"It would be nice not to live in fear," Adam added. "We don't know what that's like."

"I showed you a little of what it should have been like," Blake said. "When this is over, we'll figure out how to have all of us together in the same area."

"Are you seriously saying we could all live in Willow Bend?" Deanna asked, eyebrows arched. She laughed. "He would never allow it! Besides, once the government finds out where and what we are, they'll swoop in and scoop us all up. We'll be lab rats once again."

"Not if I can help it," Wyatt said.

Deanna noted Wyatt's muscles tighten. She knew by the look on his face he meant every word he said. While trust was starting to be earned, it had to be proven as well.

⟨⟨⟩⟩

"HONEY, would you please get your old dad a cup of coffee?" Professor Roth asked. "I have a lot of work to do."

"Sure." Alex Murphy, former secretary to Wyatt, walked through the living room heading into the kitchen. "What do you want for dinner?"

"What do you feel like making?"

"I could make a veggie-chicken casserole medley?" Alex offered, tucking a portion of her blond hair behind her ear.

"Sounds good. Thank you." As Alex went back into the kitchen, Professor Roth called to her, "Alex, have you heard from your contacts as to what is going on with the kids lately?"

"Officer Taylor called today to tell me they woke Deanna and Adam," she said from the kitchen, pulling vegetables from the refrigerator.

"What happened?"

"Officer Clark also texted. He said they left the hospital with Wyatt, Holly, and Blake this morning."

The Professor sighed impatiently. "And?"

"Nothing else."

"Did they leave Willow Bend? Are they staying at Hope and Ben's house? Wyatt's House? What's going on?"

"No idea. They both said Wyatt took some time off. He accrued quite a lot of vacation time over the years, so he could be gone for months. Once he stopped going to the station, I lost track."

"What good are you?" Professor snapped.

"Daddy…" Alex crossed her arms while leaning on the doorway. "You don't really mean that. I know you love me."

"I do," he relented. "You're the spitting image of your mother. She was one of the few people in this world I actually loved and liked…you are the other."

"All those other kids mean nothing to you?" Alex questioned.

"They're tools. Nothing more."

Alex shuddered. Heading back into the kitchen, she

mentioned over her shoulder, "Dinner will be ready in about an hour."

"Sounds good. Thank you, love!" He got on the computer to email his people still in Willow Bend, demanding information.

⟨⟩⟨⟩⟨⟩⟨⟩

BEN STRUGGLED TO SEE CLEARLY. They'd injected him with a vile of an amber substance for over a week. He knew it was slowly killing him. The hallucinations were getting stronger. It was getting more difficult to breathe every day. He often felt disoriented, and he struggled to remember things he should know. He could remember situations from long ago, but his short-term memory stumbled.

Shaking his head, he hoped they would stop this madness soon. *Madness!* That's what he felt. It was like he was slowly going mad. Hearing a scream from another room, he instantly recognized it as Hope. *Hope! Was it really her or another maddening vision?*

"Hope!" he called out.

"Ben!" she screeched. "They're everywhere! Spiders and scorpions are everywhere! I can't get away from them! Help me!"

"Hope, it's not real," he shouted back. "Everything you see is not real. Do you hear me?"

Her response was a scream of such an intensity he never wished to hear again.

"Hope! Listen to my voice!" he instructed. "Think of Blake and Holly. Imagine when we took them on outings. Stay there. Focus on that. Do not think about your fears. Do you hear me? Do not focus on your fears! Focus on God, Blake, Holly, and Wyatt!"

Not hearing a response, he assumed she wished the nightmares away and fell into the deep bliss of sleep that often took

over after the visions. Knowing Hope was there, his fears esca-
lated, imagining what they would do to her. He understood this
entire situation was a result of his idea to take Blake and Holly.
He hoped with every bone in his body Hope would not have to
pay the price for his actions.

NO TIME TO LOSE

"Keep your eyes on the stars and your feet on the ground."
Theodore Roosevelt

"What can we do to help them?" Linsey asked, as the group sat at their booth in Willow's Bend Diner on Sunday after church.

"Pray," Tanya said.

"What else? I feel like there should be more we can do. They're going to get killed."

"Shh!" Colby hushed her. "Say it a little louder. I don't think everyone in town heard you yet!"

"You know, I'll bet we can find a rodeo going on right now," Shawn suggested with a sly smile.

Megan rolled her eyes. "How is that going to help them?"

"We have to travel to the rodeos," Shawn hinted. "We do it all the time. You guys could come with us this time."

"Again. How is this going to help?" Megan asked.

Shawn groaned, dropping his head onto his hand. "Megan, I

love you, but there are days where I don't think the elevator connects to the top floor." He sighed. "You're a genius, but I sometimes question your street smarts."

Taking her hand into his, Mac gently explained, "Think about it, Meg. Just because we say we're going to a rodeo, doesn't mean we're actually going to the rodeo. Let's say there's a rodeo up in Wyoming. We take off and make a right turn in Arkansas heading toward Maine."

"That's dishonest," Megan objected.

"How else are we going to help them?" Shawn asked. "I can't see you going to your parents and asking, *Can I go help Holly and Blake rescue their parents and siblings from an evil tyrant?* Pretty sure they would lock you in your room and throw away the key."

"Probably. That's because they love me and want me safe."

"I'm sure."

"Is there another option?" Colby asked. "I don't want to be grounded until I'm eighteen, or worse yet, charged with some crime along the way."

"What crime?" Tanya asked.

"Let's see – breaking and entering, kidnapping, attempted murder, accessory to murder, aiding and abetting…I could go on," Colby said. Colby's dad was a police officer, so he was familiar with the terminology. "They're going up there to break into a facility and break their siblings free of their father and get them loose of that man. These are the dictionary definitions for kidnapping, along with breaking and entering. In the process, they may kill guards, nurses, or even Professor Roth. If we help them, these charges are viable options for us as well as accessories."

"I hadn't thought of it that way." Lindsey slumped in her seat. "I feel so useless. I can't stand the idea of not being able to help at all. Or worse yet, sitting here not knowing anything."

"We just started getting to know them." Mac propped his

chin on his hand. "I don't want to sit here and wait to see if they come back or not. I want to do something."

For the fifth time that day, Colby pulled out his phone to check the email account they set up before they left. "They still haven't emailed." Colby shook his head. "What they're doing is dangerous. There's a reason they don't have phones, and are using an autonomous GPS."

"We can help. We're strong," Shawn said.

"You saw how she flung those men with a wave of her hand. There are four in the sibling group with that gift," Colby pointed out. "You may be strong. I may be strong. We've gotten in enough fights to know we're good fighters. However, we are nothing compared to that group! Blake told us about the others in their sibling group. There are telekinetics, telepaths, and another who is an empath like Blake. There's even a mind reader, and one whose mind works so quickly that he's almost a precog. They are Blake and Holly's equal. We are not."

"That was blunt," Megan said.

"That's the reality of what they're fixin' to walk into. That's not even including the big guys with guns," Colby said. "We seriously cannot even remotely add to their power or skill. We are only your basic, everyday human."

"That doesn't mean we can't help," Lindsey argued. "They're human too. They can die just as easily as we can. The only difference is they have an extra gene or two."

"Lindsey, what can you do to help?" Colby challenged. "Have you taken a good look at yourself?"

"Have *you* taken a good look at me?" Lindsey asked. She turned to Mac, who was on her other side, and slid closer to him. Setting her hand on the side of his face, she ran her fingers down to his chest as she rested her head on his shoulder. His face flushed red, while Megan narrowed her eyes at Lindsey. "Mac," Lindsey purred, "would you do me a huge favor?"

When she ran her fingers down his chest toward his thigh, he jumped. "Lindsey, you need to stop," he warned, grabbing her hand.

"Just proving my point," she said, sitting up. "Just because I'm short, don't judge me. I have a myriad of talents you haven't even seen yet!"

"Lindsey, don't ruin yourself to prove a point," Shawn said, clenching his jaw. "You tend to take things to extremes."

Mac arched his eyebrows. "Jealous?"

"No."

"Is there a reason you don't want me to do something like that?" Lindsey pressed.

"You're like a sister to me. Don't do something you'll regret just because you don't see your true value," Shawn explained.

"What does that mean?"

"Lindsey, I see you trying too hard to get the attention of guys," Shawn continued. "You think shaking your pom-poms or being sexy is how you get a guy. Did you ever see Holly do that?"

"No," Lindsey said.

"What about Tanya or Megan?"

"No, but to be fair –"

"To be fair…what?" Tanya leaned forward. "Go ahead and finish that sentence." She and Lindsey locked eyes momentarily before Tanya pointed out, "I'm the one who's dating Blake. I didn't have to shake my pom-poms or try to be something I'm not to impress him. When are you going to learn that a guy should like you for who you are, not who you project?"

"What does that mean?" Lindsey asked.

"You're cute," Tanya said. "However, you use your looks to get guys who only want you for your looks and body. It's like you want them to objectify you. You're smarter than this."

"Megan's smart, and I don't see her dating," Lindsey argued.

"I have goals and standards," Megan defended herself. "I have my eye on someone in particular. I'm not going to settle."

"What if he doesn't want you?"

Megan shrugged. "If he doesn't, that's his loss. I'm not going to be someone I'm not just so he notices me."

"Who is it?" Mac asked. "I haven't seen you look even remotely interested in anyone."

"He'll have to figure it out for himself," Megan said coyly.

"Maybe he's dense."

When he said that, Megan burst out in laughter. Mac was the one who held her interest. He basically called himself dense.

"What's so funny?" Mac asked.

"If he doesn't figure it out, then he's not as smart as I gave him credit for."

"Men are not mind readers," Shawn jumped back into the conversation. "Sometimes, we need a hint or two."

"He has some work to do before I would consider going out with him anyway," Megan said with a shrug.

"What kind of work?" Shawn asked, intrigued.

"Heart work. He didn't used to be the way he is now."

"People change," Mac said.

"Right. They go through their growth phases both physically, mentally, and emotionally," Megan explained. "He needs to grow in all areas."

Mac furrowed his brow. "Is he short?"

"Don't hurt yourself trying to figure it out," Megan teased. "My love life is not the main topic of conversation here."

"Neither is my behavior," Lindsey challenged.

"Actually, yes, it is," Tanya countered. "If you go in there thinking you can weasel information or access with your body, that's a problem. You have more assets than you give yourself credit for."

Lindsey toyed with her napkin. "It's all a moot point since we're not going to do anything."

"There are other things we can do." Tanya pulled a piece of paper from her back pocket with a list of questions that plagued her since Blake left with the others. "There are some questions that need answers."

"Such as?" Colby asked.

"What happened to Alex Murphy?" Tanya asked. "She disappeared right after Deanna and Adam arrived in town. We need to figure out who she really is."

"True," Colby said, considering it. "What else?"

"We know there are boxes of information in Ben's workshop about the clinic. I gave Blake a file on Professor Roth and the other campuses he owns from there."

"There are other campuses?" Shawn asked, taken aback.

"Yes. There's a lot of information we don't know. We can use our time wisely in order to help them," Tanya explained. "We can research the crap out of Professor Noah Roth, the clinics he owns, and any other experiments or organizations his name is attached to. We don't need to waste our time just waiting to hear from them. There's no time to lose. If they contact us, we need to be ready with valuable information for them. The more information they have, the better off they'll be."

"You mean like getting the schematics of the buildings?" Megan asked.

"You can do that?" Mac asked, amazed.

"The internet is chockfull of valuable intel if you know where to look," Megan said, wiggling her eyebrows.

"Can you show me?" Mac asked.

"Definitely!"

"Let's break into teams," Tanya proposed. "Mac and Megan, you two lose yourselves in a computer. Find schematics of the clinics if you can, also anything you can find about the clinics, and information on Professor Roth."

"Sounds good," Megan said, while Mac nodded in response.

"Lindsey and Shawn, do you think you two can go to the library and look at old records and microfiche on anything and everything you can find about Professor Noah Roth, or any other places or organizations he's connected to, without killing each other?" Tanya asked.

"I reckon we can be good for the sake of the mission," Shawn agreed.

Linsey nodded. "Yes."

"Good. Also, both teams see what you can find out about Alexandra Murphy. That leaves Colby and me to dive into the boxes in Ben's workshop," Tanya said. "We'll be limited to whatever Ben found, but there is a lot of information there."

"Fair enough," Colby agreed. "We can do that. Stay in contact with each other. Then, when they do get ahold of us, we can give them all the information we found."

"Is it safe to transfer information electronically?" Megan asked.

"We'll cross that bridge when we get to it," Tanya said.

⊲▯⊲▯⊲▯⊲▯

"At least he keeps it organized," Colby said, as he and Tanya walked into Ben's workshop after he picked the lock.

Tanya turned on the shop light. "Let's hope he keeps his records area clean and organized, too."

"You have a flashlight?" Colby asked.

"Yeah. Here." She handed it to him. "The light's on, though. Why do you need a flashlight?"

"Spiders don't care if the light's on or not. They're still making webs. The flashlight reflects off webs better."

Tanya raised an eyebrow. "A big guy like you is afraid of spiders?"

"You do know we have black widows and brown recluse here?"

"Yes. However, for the most part, most of our spiders take care of those gargantuan mosquitos we love so much. You know, like the wolf spiders. They're our friends."

17

Colby shuddered. "I don't care. The wolf spider nests are the creepiest. Have you seen the funnels they create?"

"At least they're easy to spot," Tanya said, as Colby killed a spider in the web.

Digging through tools, boxes, totes, camping gear, and gardening equipment, they finally found the boxes they were looking for after about two hours of moving things around and Colby killing several spiders.

"He really wanted to hide these," Colby said, moving the boxes by two out from behind the piles.

"Do we want to look at them here or take them somewhere else?" Tanya asked, with a box in her arms.

"I don't think anywhere is safe."

"How much money do you have?" she asked.

Colby cocked his head to the side. "Why? What are you thinking?"

"I think we should regroup and store everything in a hotel room."

"They can still track that. They can track anything we do. If we rent a storage unit, they can track that too."

"What can we do? We know they're watching the houses. They're probably waiting to see what we come out with," Tanya said.

"You think?"

"I'm surprised they haven't barged in here."

"I would accuse you of being paranoid, but we need to be paranoid in this situation."

"Whatever we find in these boxes that is useful, we need to disguise it, take pictures of it with our phones, and –"

"No," Colby cut her off. He ran out to his truck and returned with a digital camera. "We need to keep as much as we can offline."

"Now, who's paranoid?"

"As I said, we need to be paranoid in this situation. This man has killed a lot of people and gotten away with it. He has a lot of power and money behind him."

"Then let's be the mosquito in his tent," Tanya said with a sly smile.

◆◆◆◆◆

"WHAT'S this microfiche stuff Tanya's talking about?" Mac asked as he and Megan drove to the library in Mac's car. The hours for the library were cut to six o'clock at night for Sunday, but they still had a few good hours to do research.

"They're tiny pictures of old newspapers, articles, catalogs, files, and photographs. You have to look at it on a special machine to read it."

"Do they still use that stuff?"

"Yes. When microfiche was first created, they converted everything to microfiche to make it easier to store. When computers came around, they converted a lot over, but there's a lot they didn't convert due to cost," Megan explained.

"You've used it?"

"Yep. When doing research."

"I thought computers were your thing."

"They are. There are other ways of collecting information in the world besides computers. Don't get me wrong, they're a great resource. You can't rely on everything you read on the internet, though. Some things have been tainted by those with power and money. The microfiche is permanent. It can't be altered. It can be destroyed, but not altered."

"Good point."

"So, when you need to research something, how do you do it?" she asked.

He shrugged. "Google."

"When you're learning a new trick, or are wanting to learn how to do something, how or who do you go to?"

"If it's a trick, I go to the person I think can best get me to the best person possible. If I want to learn something, I head over to the internet. Undoubtedly, someone has done an instruction video on it."

"Okay. Let's say you want to create a new way of doing something."

"By this point, everything has already been done at least once."

"Nope."

"How can you say that?"

Megan rolled her eyes. "If everyone thought like you, we would be stuck in the dark ages."

"How do you figure?"

"Well, they once thought the earth was flat. They also tried many times to take flight before the Wright brothers got into the air. And if they stopped there, we wouldn't have massive airplanes, jet fighters, or space shuttles. We wouldn't have world access or even space flight. The magical question of *what if?* has propelled many new adventures. Some inventors were way ahead of their time. Tesla and Einstein were amazing! If things stopped after Tesla was killed, then we would be stuck in 1943. What if we stopped developing new guns after Samuel Colt received his first patten in 1836? Many inventions can be improved upon. Many ideas came as a spring-board of another *what if?* question."

"That's an interesting way to look at it. Anyone ever tell you that you have a unique way of looking at the world?"

"All the time. I don't mind. I take it as a compliment. I don't think like everyone else. I'm not a drone. I'm an original," she said proudly.

"How do you do it?" he asked.

"Do what?"

"How do you go against the mainstream? How do you go against your friends at times? Isn't it lonely?"

"At times," Megan admitted. "But I would rather answer to God for my behavior, then care what the world thinks."

"Wow."

"What?"

"That's quite a statement!"

"If I were to die today, I know I've done my best to follow God and His Word. Can you say the same thing?"

Not making eye contact as he focused on the road, he admitted, "Don't know."

"God created this world solely with His voice. Can you imagine what Judgement Day will look like when you stand before Him to answer for your life choices? The kicker? When you marry, you're responsible for your spouse and children's choices as well. The man is the head of the household. He is supposed to treat the wife as Christ treated the church. Are you treating girls the way Christ wants you to?"

Mac squirmed in his seat. "Enough."

"Getting a little too close to home?" Megan observed.

"We gave Colby a lot of grief."

"For making the right choices?" Megan asked. "Really?"

"Yes. He puts up with our antics. If I were to not behave the way I normally do, Shawn might not want me to be his partner."

"Do you answer to Shawn or to God? Last time I checked, Shawn wasn't God."

"He's not, but –"

"But nothing. Who do you answer to, Mac? Is it Shawn or God? Who's your true judge?"

Mac sighed as they pulled into the library. When they got out of the car, he mumbled, "Guess I have some thinking to do."

"Guess you do," Megan said, walking purposely toward the doors of the library. "In the meantime, we have friends who need to help."

❖❖❖❖

WHILE MEGAN WORKED on the computer, Mac pulled a few microfiches to look through, more out of curiosity than anything. Meanwhile, Lindsey and Shawn stopped for a few snacks before arriving at the library.

Taking off his backpack from his shoulder, Shawn sat down next to Mac. "Whatcha looking at?"

"This is microfiche," Mac said. "I'm looking for any old articles on the clinic from Maine."

"Isn't that our job?"

"Well, you weren't here. Have at it." Mac stood and went over to where Megan was on a computer. "Shawn and Lindsey are here for the microfiche and article assignment."

"Good. We need to get out of here," Megan said, logging off the computer.

Picking up her backpack for her, Mac asked, "Where are we going?"

"I printed a few articles, but we need to go deeper. I have a set-up in my basement that'll allow me to do what I need to do and go where I want to go."

"Sounds good."

"Where are you two going?" Linsey asked, seeing the pair walking toward the door.

"We're heading back to my house. You two have this end covered," Megan said. "Dig deep."

"How deep?"

"We have to go into the dark web to find what I need," Megan explained. "Be careful, but dig deep. What you're looking for can only be found on microfiche. It won't be on a search engine."

Running over to the printer, Megan ignored Linsey's objections. "What's her problem?" Lindsey asked.

"She smells a mystery. And you know Megan. When there's a problem she can't solve…" Mac's voice faded.

"We're in trouble," Lindsey said, watching her.

When Megan returned, she and Mac left the library.

Lindsey sat down beside Shawn. "Find anything yet?" she asked.

"No. This is what Mac was looking at," Shawn explained. "It seems Professor Noah Roth made the news way back when. He was a big deal. These are from a New York City newspaper," he said, gesturing toward the articles.

"Megan said we need to dig deep," Lindsey said. "We're going to have to look in some not-so-obvious places."

"Meaning?"

"Don't look at the big papers. Look for articles, journals, or newspapers in Maine, mainly near where they're located."

"Didn't Wyatt say that was somewhere near a park?" Shawn asked.

"God help me if you're ever in charge of finding me," Linsey said on a sigh as she got on the computer. Scanning the list of parks, she found it. "Here. It's near this – Rangeley Plantation."

"So, do we just dive in, looking for anything coinciding with Professor Roth in this plantation area?"

Linsey dropped her head on her hands, shaking it. "How do you do research for your reports. Didn't you learn anything in class?"

"I always have one of the girls do the research for me."

Lindsey huffed. "Of course you did." Shaking her head under her breath she added, "How did I ever like you?"

"What do you mean?" Shawn asked.

"You have the intelligence quotient of a doorknob." Standing, Linsey added, "You think the world is here for your enjoyment. You think every girl likes you."

He crossed his arms. "You do."

"Bless your delusional little heart."

"You like me. You can deny it all you want to, but you know it's true."

"Correction. I did."

"Fine. Then Blake came, and you're suddenly falling all over him."

"Blake has looks, heart, and the brains to match. He likes Tanya, though."

"Probably because she knows who she is and isn't trying to throw herself at every cute guy."

"You have a lot of nerve!" Linsey said, getting into his face. "You behave the same way. You chase after any girl who remotely looks at you. Just because you're a guy doesn't make it better."

"As a girl, you have quite a reputation," Shawn said quietly.

"As a guy, you do too. You will never know what it's like to have a girl like me. You are a cretin of the highest level. I don't know what I ever saw in you."

Shawn sighed, shaking his head. "Is that supposed to hurt me? Because it doesn't."

"Is there a problem?" a librarian walked up to the pair and asked. "You two are making a scene in a place where you should be quiet. If you persist, I'll ask you to leave."

"I'm sorry," Shawn said. "We'll be quiet."

"Sorry," Linsey apologized.

"Please be more respectful," she said and left.

"Are you finished?" Shawn hissed.

"Yes. Are you?" Lindsey whispered back.

"Yes. We need to do this in order to help Blake and Holly. We don't have time to work through our issues. Basically, I don't like you, and you don't like me. That's not important right now. We have to work together to do our assignment. Can you do it without sarcasm?"

"Hopefully."

"Fine. Have it your way. You do it your way, and I'll do it mine," he said. Turning toward the librarian who was walking away, Shawn made a beeline for her. "Madam," he started.

"Shawn, I've known you since you were two years old. There is no need to call me madam," the librarian corrected him.

"Fair enough. Cybil, would you be willing to help me out?" he asked, flashing his brilliant smile.

"Anytime, Shawn. What do you need?"

"How would one go about finding information regarding a professor from over thirty years ago?"

Wide-eyed, she exclaimed, "Oh, dear! From around here?"

"No. It's a professor up in the Vermont and New Hampshire area."

"Obscure," she observed. "All of the records are on the computer. Enter The Professor's name and location. The computer will cross-reference your searches and tell you anytime that particular professor is mentioned."

"Awesome. You're an angel."

"I'm not doing it for you." Cybil looked at him over the top of her glasses. She knew him too well. "You have to do your own homework. You have a habit of roping in the younger girls in the library to help you. Not happening today. If I see you trying to get someone else to do your work, I'll kick you out of here myself. I don't care if Aiden hates me for it or not."

"Aiden's a good kid."

"He is. And he admires your skill in roping."

Leaning forward, he quietly asked, "What if I offer him some extra help in exchange for some extra help of yours on this project?"

"Shawn," she warned.

"Fine. Can't blame a guy for trying. I'll give Aiden a hand at the next rodeo anyway. Tell him to find me at the next one he comes to where we're there too."

"Thank you. Your help is appreciated," Cybil said with a smile. "You're still on your own."

"I get it. Just looking out for the kid. If he screws up, he could get himself hurt."

"Thank you," she said appreciatively.

Making his way to the computer in the library, he sighed heavily. He was losing his touch. He was certain part of that was due to Lindsey's attitude. He could feel the anger pulsating off her from across the library. He and Lindsey would need to work their issues out sooner or later. If he had his way, it would be sooner.

"Life is really simple, but we insist on making it complicated." Confucius

*A*lex paced her office. Not having any information to give her dad could prove dangerous. She called everyone she could think of with no success. As she sat in her seat, her intercom went off.

"Alex?" The Professor's voice crackled over the intercom. "Please come to my office?"

"Yes, sir," Alex responded.

She would never get over the nerves and anxiety she felt every time she was called to his office. She may seem confident on the outside, but inside she was a nervous wreck.

"Hey, Alex," Security Officer Rick Miller acknowledged her as they passed in the hallway.

She gave him a curt nod. "Miller."

She relished the time she had in Willow Bend and longed to

return. She really wanted to go to the basement and check on Ben.

Taking a deep breath, she knocked on the door.

"Enter," came The Professor's voice.

When Alex walked in, he gestured to the seat opposite him. The vastness of the study, yet the cramped feel to it, never ceased to amaze her. She often felt intimidated by the sheer volume of information in the study and knew most of it was top secret. The walls were lined with bookshelves that were jam-packed with books and binders. His mahogany desk was bigger than she thought he would need but always seemed cluttered. The leather chairs and sofa had folders and binders stacked on them. Some day she knew she would have to go through it all when her dad passed, and she was not looking forward to it. She fully understood what her father did and the actions he took over the years.

When she sat, he said, "I have tried to get information, but no one has any. What do your contacts say?"

"Just what I told you this morning. After he left, there was no tracking him."

"What about via his mobile?"

"He didn't take his cell phone with him."

"Hmm," The Professor said, stroking his chin. "Seems he's onto us. We need to be just as wise in our moves."

"What do you mean by moves?" Alex asked.

"This is like a game of chess. There are moves and counter moves. In the game of chess, there are also certain people who are expendable, like the pawns. There's the bishop, who represents our nurses. Some can be expendable, but I really need them to care for the rooks."

"The rooks?"

"The rooks represent the children. The knights are those on security. The knights and the bishops care for the rooks. The rooks are what they're protecting because they protect us," he said, pointing to himself and Alex. "We're the king and queen."

"I see," Alex said, shifting uncomfortably. "I've never thought of myself as a queen. If any piece I felt represented me, it was the knight."

"You are indeed a warrior, and a formidable one at that, but you are anything but expendable, my darling. You are one of the few things I care most about in this world."

"And," she nervously cleared her throat, "where do the Willow Bend people fit in?"

"They're the white side of the chessboard. Our job is to annihilate them," he said sternly. "I need you to focus."

"Yes, sir."

"They're bringing the game to us. Mark me. They are heading this way. We need to be ready."

"I thought Deanna and Adam were bringing Holly and Blake back?"

"I am certain they are in their own way. I think Wyatt feels they trust him, so he is driving them all right to our front door."

"What are you going to do when they get here?"

"Whatever I have to. Those children are all mine. I do not care what Hope and Ben told them. They will join us."

⟨⟩⟨⟩

AFTER ALEX'S meeting with her dad, she wandered the halls for a few moments. Being *the queen* gave her free reign in movement throughout the complex. That's when she saw Rick Miller on Security. Now was her chance to see Ben!

"Rick," Alex flashed a brilliant smile while her brown eyes twinkled.

He grinned. "Alex! I'm surprised you actually remembered my first name. You usually call me by my last name."

"I know. I don't always like to be so formal. I need you to give me the keys to the isolation rooms. I'll bring them back to you when I'm finished."

"I have to get clearance from your dad," he said, picking up his radio. Before she had a chance to object, Rick said, "819 to Professor."

"Go ahead," she heard her dad's voice come across, and she caught her breath.

"Alex is here, she's asking –"

"Officer Miller," The Professor's tone was sharp. "Are you seriously questioning something my daughter is asking you to do?"

"N-no sir," Rick mumbled. "Sorry to disturb you."

"This is an order to anyone within earshot of these radios. My daughter has all rights and authority as if it is coming directly from me. Is that understood?"

"Yes, sir," Rick said and replaced his radio on his clip. "Sorry, Alex."

"I didn't mean to get you into trouble. I was going to stop you, but you moved too fast."

"Thanks for trying. Here are the keys. Give me a call when and where you want to meet to get them back to me. I'll just notate it in my journal, so I don't get in trouble for not having my keys when asked."

"Fair enough." Alex nodded, accepting the keys. Looking at her watch, she offered, "Just meet me in the cafeteria in about thirty minutes? Let me buy you lunch to make up for getting you into trouble?"

"Really?" His face brightened. "That would be great!"

"See you in thirty," she said and left. As soon as she got to the stairwell, she ran down the few flights to the basement. Unlocking the door, she crinkled her nose. The smell always got to her down here.

She checked the handle of door number one. When it gave way, she moved onto door number two, knowing no one was in there. Door number two had the same result, so she moved to door number three. When it opened, she sighed. "Come on!" she whispered to herself. "Where are you?"

When door number four's latch didn't budge, she used the keys to open the door. "Hope!" she said, stunned. "What did they do to you?" she asked, running into the room. Resting her hands on either side of her face, she said, "I'm so sorry."

"Get me out of here," Hope begged, tears pouring down her cheeks.

"I can't. I'm sorry. There are too many guards for even me to pull something like that off. Know Wyatt and the kids are on their way, though."

"You're going to leave me in here? Do you know what they're doing to us?"

"Us? Where's Ben?"

"He's down a few doors." Hope narrowed her eyes at Alex. "You're seriously going to leave us with that sadistic father of yours? You were our friend!"

"I still am! Honestly, you guys are probably the only true friends I ever had," she confessed.

"And this is how you thank us? With friends like you, who needs enemies?"

"Hope, you can't mean that."

"Try me!"

"I'm sorry. Please forgive me," she said and left Hope, locking the door behind her amidst Hope's yells and screams.

She checked the door right next to Hope, but it was empty. Unlocking the next door, she was not prepared for what she saw. "Oh, Ben!" Her heart broke. Ben's clothes were covered in blood. He was coated in sweat, bruises, and scrapes.

"Alex?" he asked, squinting at her. "Are you really here?"

She went in and crouched in front of him. Brushing her hand on his cheek, she said, "I'm so sorry."

"Get these ties off, so we can get Hope and get out of here."

"I'm sorry. I can't."

"Alex! Cut me loose! Stop messing around!"

"I'm not messing around. I can't."

"What? Why not?"

"I can't. I told Hope I couldn't either. Wyatt and the kids are on their way. We need to wait for them. Please wait for them? They're coming. Once they're here, I can do something."

"Why are you here? How did you get here? Why isn't Wyatt with you right now?"

Alex looked down, ashamed. "Professor Roth is my dad," she mumbled.

"He's *what*? *What* did you just say?" Ben demanded, fire in his eyes.

"I said, he's my dad," she said a little louder. When her eyes met his, she shuddered. The hatred was unmistakable.

"You were spying for him? This whole time? Really? What is wrong with you? We invited you into our family! We accepted you as one of our own! This whole time, you were a wolf in sheep's clothing!"

"I-I'm sorry! I had to! You have to understand –"

"Nothing! I don't have to understand a single thing!" Ben snapped. "Leave!"

"Ben, I-I honestly love you! I know you love me too!"

"I loved who you were, yes," he said coolly. "But I have no idea who you really are!"

"I was myself when I was in Willow Bend. There was no pretense. Please?" she begged. "I need you to know that I love you."

He leaned forward so his face was less than a few inches from hers. He enunciated every word, as he said, "Do not ever come near my family or me again. If I see you anywhere near them, there will be nothing on this planet that will be able to protect you!"

"You can't mean that," Alex said, tears falling down her cheeks. "I really am the person I was in Willow Bend."

"Yes, and then you went home every night and probably filled daddy in on our every move."

"I –"

"NO!" Ben roared. "No! Do not even try! You are a Judas. You wormed your way into our lives, knowing you were betraying us the entire time. Did you know Adam and Deanna were on their way?"

"Yes," she admitted. "He made me return here when they arrived."

"Did you tell him Wyatt and Hope were close?"

"I knew they were close," she admitted. "Yes. I told him."

"Did you tell him you and I were close?"

Alex caught her breath as she looked into his eyes. "I didn't tell him we kissed. I only told him we were close."

"I should have never let you in." Looking toward the ceiling, he said, "Lord Jesus, this is all my fault. Please protect everyone through this. Take me, instead of the innocents."

Alex covered her mouth. "Stop it! You're not going to die."

"Yes. I am. Your father is literally killing me, Alex! Did you know that? Do you have any idea what he's been injecting into us?"

"No," she admitted.

"Poison. Pure poison! Yes, taking the kids was my idea. However, it's your fault we're here. If anything happens to any of us, it will be on your conscience. Your choices have ramifications. I'm paying for mine right now. But you? You have to live with this mess you caused. We were nice to you. We befriended you. Just like Judas betrayed Jesus with a kiss, you betrayed us." He sighed, looking back toward the ceiling again. "I now know what it felt like. I'm so sorry, Jesus!"

"Ben, please stop?" Alex begged. "You're breaking my heart."

He leaned forward again and hissed, "I may be breaking your heart, but you shattered ours! Your father is killing us! I can only imagine what these rooms were used for in the past. Don't be naïve, Alex. Your dad is no saint! I wouldn't be surprised if he was related to Lucifer himself!"

"Ben," she breathed out, as her face paled.

"Leave, Alex. Don't look back. Live your life, knowing what you've done."

Alex stood. Shaking her head, she covered her mouth, unable to say anything.

"I said to leave! Go spend your money, Judas! Don't know the story? Look it up! You betrayed us all!"

She flinched at his words. "I love you."

Ben spit at her. She took a step back, so it barely missed her shoes.

"Leave," Ben growled, and she jumped. "Do not ever come back! Do you hear me? Don't come back!" he shouted.

She glanced at him one more time as she closed the door. He was seething in his chair. Fury was a tame word for what he looked like while he continued to shout at her to leave. Once the door was closed, she rested against the door, trying to control her tears. "I'm sorry, Ben," she whispered, still hearing his rant. "I'm so sorry."

⊕⊕⊕⊕

RIDING in the passenger's seat of the van relatively in silence, except for the radio, was getting to Blake. About an hour into the trip, he leaned down and pulled out some folders from his backpack. "Here," he said, passing them back to Adam and Deanna.

"What's this?" Adam asked, handing half the folders to Deanna.

"Some light reading." Blake shrugged. "You want to learn more about The Professor. Here you go. These are copies of files my dad got before he and my mom rescued us so long ago."

"Interesting," Adam said, opening a file. The first thing he saw were photos of mutilated babies. In flipping through the files, he learned of the many trials and failures of Professor Roth. He filed these lessons learned about The Professor in his mind, adding them to the many facts he learned about him over the years. "If I know The Professor as well as I think I do, he's probably keeping Hope and Ben alive for now. He wants them to suffer. He wants to torture them for taking something of his."

"That's disturbing," Holly commented as she looked over the shoulder of Deanna and Adam at the folder's contents.

"He is disturbing," Adam agreed and then added, "even sadistic."

"How did you guys not rebel?" Holly asked. "He hurt you and your best friend."

"It's called Stockholm Syndrome," Wyatt said over his shoulder.

"No," Deanna said. "Ours was a matter of survival. We don't trust him. We don't really like him. We owe him because he gave us life and raised us. We tolerate his ruthless behavior because we know the power he holds. It's not out of loyalty. It's survival."

"What if you had a different choice? Would you take it?" Holly asked.

"In a heartbeat," Deanna said. Then she added, "As long as it doesn't land us in the hands of the government."

"I think we can do that," Wyatt said confidently.

"Can you guarantee it?" she challenged.

"I'll bet we can help find you all homes to keep you safe. If you're spread throughout the area, yet close enough to help each other, would that work?"

"How can you offer that?"

"Being a county sheriff, I have my connections," Wyatt explained. "I know many within the system who would be willing to lend a hand or help us establish what we need to in order to get y'all settled."

"You would do that?"

"Yep."

Narrowing her eyes, she asked, "Why?"

"I told you that you're family. In the south, family is everything. We may not necessarily like each other, but don't you dare let anyone outside of the family come against another family member. Blood means something in the south. Family means everything."

"How are we a family?" Adam asked. "You are in no way related to us."

"Hope is my fiancé," Wyatt said, focusing on the road as he periodically glanced in the rearview mirror. "We were supposed to be married on the day y'all came crashing into town."

"I'm sorry," Deanna apologized. "We didn't know. The Professor told us as soon as you were separated to move in."

"I appreciate the apology. I forgive you. We just need to rescue the woman I love. We also need to rescue your brothers and sisters."

"How are we related, though?" Adam asked. "Hope isn't Holly's real mother."

"She is for all intents and purposes," Wyatt countered. "She raised Blake and Holly. She is their mother. I will marry Hope. At that point, Holly and Blake will be my step-children. They are your brother and sister. Therefore, we are family. At least close enough, anyway."

"I'm struggling with the idea of Holly and Blake being considered my brother and sister," Deanna admitted.

"Just because we were raised away from each other doesn't make us any less siblings," Holly pointed out. "I want to learn more about you. I want to learn what you like and what you dislike. Your hobbies and your horrors. Your dreams and your desires."

"What hobbies do you have?" Adam asked.

"Well, I like to garden, write —"

"Write what?" Adam cut her off.

"I write stories and like to journal."

"What kind of stories?"

"Really good ones," Blake jumped in. "She writes them, and then I play them out in our minds."

Adam looked from Holly to Blake, eyebrows arched. "Your minds are linked?"

"Yes."

"But," he turned back to Holly, "you're not a telepath."

"Blake and I have always had a strong connection," Holly explained. "We know what each other are thinking without having to say anything."

"I think it has something to do with growing up the way we did," Blake said. "We were inseparable. We did everything together."

"Even schooling. We always work together as a team," Holly added.

"They only had to look at each other to figure out what the other was thinking," Wyatt agreed. "You could see it in their faces. No words needed."

"Then, on the day you found us, I thought something, and she heard what I thought," Blake continued. "It was the first time that happened."

"He could already hear what I thought," Holly said, "but before that day, I couldn't hear what he thought."

"And now?" Adam asked.

"We can," Blake confirmed.

"So, if we were to separate you by several rooms, could you understand each other?" Adam asked.

"We did it in the hospital once her head cleared," Blake explained. "When she was finally off the pain medicine, I was down in the cafeteria with Tanya, and she was in the room with Colby. She asked me to bring up another order of fries…her weakness."

"Ahh, so now we learn how to get you to do what we want," Deanna said with a smirk. "A good batch of fries are the way to your heart."

"And a bad batch will get it thrown in your face," Holly hinted.

"Noted," Deanna said, looking down at the file. "So, according to this file, my mother's name was Skye Jenson." Picking up the picture, she smiled. "She was pretty."

"You've never seen her before?" Blake asked. "Not even a picture?"

"No. Have you seen yours?" Deanna asked.

Blake reached into his back pocket and pulled out his wallet. Removing a picture from his wallet, he handed it to Deanna. "This is my mother. Her name was Katrina Nelson."

"She's pretty too," Deanna said, looking at the picture before handing it back to Blake. "And yours?" she asked Holly.

"My real mother's name was Hope Hunt," Holly said, pulling her mother's picture from her purse. Looking at it briefly, she then passed it on to Deanna. "This photo is her original badge picture. I guess the picture from her file is missing."

"Interesting," Deanna said, looking at it before passing it back. "They are all very pretty."

"And very much alone in this world," Adam said, handing Deanna the picture of his mother. "Mine was Andrea Williams. They either had little or no family from what I read so far."

"There isn't a homely looking one in the bunch," Deanna said, flipping through some of the other files, looking at the pictures. "Even without makeup, they were all natural beauties."

"Where did he find them?" Holly asked. "Does it say?"

"Looks mostly like colleges in the area," Deanna said, scanning the files.

Adam looked through a couple more before he handed the files he had to Deanna. "The man is a monster. What he did to those women, to our moms, was inexcusable."

"You don't know the half of it," Blake said taking another folder out of his bag. "Take a look at this," he said, handing it to Adam.

Adam's eyes widened as he scanned picture after picture of dead woman. All of them had blood coming from their eyes, nose, mouth, and ears. "This was not an accident," Adam said, appalled. "These deaths were not from natural causes. All these years, he had me study serial killers, and he's the worst one!"

Deanna glanced over at the file Adam had, equally horrified. "Holly, isn't this one your mom?" she asked, pointing toward one.

On instinct, Holly glanced at the picture. Her heart instantly shattered. That picture was now seared into her mind. The horror would not be soon forgotten.

"Holly," Wyatt said cautiously. "Holly, set the van down. We cannot afford for someone to see a flying van."

Blake reached back, pushing calm feelings toward Holly. Holly responded by reaching forward between Adam and Deanna, grabbing his hand. She took a deep breath. As she let it out, she set the van back on the ground with a thud. The tires skipped, and the van jerked before they caught on the road. Holly took a few more deep cleansing breaths to clear her head.

"May I?" Adam asked.

"May you what?" Wyatt glanced in the rearview mirror. When Adam did not initially respond, he continued, "We're on a backroad. Could you imagine if we were on a major highway right now? Holly, I need you not to do that again."

"Yes, sir," Holly mumbled, wiping the tears from her eyes.

"May I go into your mind?" Adam asked.

Blake narrowed his eyes. "What will you do?"

"Take the memory away. She doesn't need that picture cemented in her mind. It's bad enough I can't erase them. I don't want her stuck with it, too," Adam explained.

"You can do that?" Wyatt asked.

"I can do a lot. So can Blake." Adam glanced up at Blake.

"Can you show me?" Blake asked.

Adam turned to Holly. "Do you trust me enough to go into your mind?"

Wiping her eyes, she asked, "You'll take that picture away?"

"Yes."

"Holly?" Blake asked.

Holly nodded in response.

"Come up to this seat, so Blake can keep ahold of your hand," Adam said. "Blake, keep ahold of her hand so you can see inside her mind to see what I am doing."

"Deanna," Wyatt said from the driver's seat, "you'll be good while they do this, right?"

"Yes, sir," Deanna agreed.

Once Holly settled on the end of the seat next to Adam, the trio joined hands and closed their eyes. Holly saw different flashes of her memories swirling around them before they stood in what looked to be a completely white room with no doors or windows. The walls, floor, and ceiling all looked like they were made of large, white, rectangle tiles.

"Where's the memory?" Adam asked Holly, while Adam, Blake, and Holly continued to hold hands.

Holly shook her head, tears crawling down her cheeks. "I knew in my head what he did, but to actually see it was too much. I have the picture of her ID. To me, seeing her smile, I was able to create stories. Stories where she laughed and played. Stories where she was happy. To see how it ended is just too much."

"I need you to tell me where you put it," he said, glancing around the empty room. "This room is white, for innocence. Where's your black room?"

"What black room?" Blake asked.

"White is innocence," Adam explained. "She wants to remain here. She doesn't want to look at the dark room."

"What's the dark room?" Blake asked.

"It's black. It looks just like this, only completely black," Adam said. "The black room holds the darkness. It holds the evil things of this world she does not want to face or look at. Holly's heart is pure. She wants to remain here. Professor Roth lives in the black room. They could not be more opposite."

"How do we find this black room?" Blake asked.

"Holly." Adam nodded toward her. "She has to show it to us. Where is it, Holly?"

Holly shook her head. "I don't want to look in there."

"Holly, I can calm you," Blake offered. "We really need to find the room to take the memory away."

"I don't want to let it go," Holly said. "When I find Professor Roth, I want him to understand what it felt like to see that picture."

"Holly, this isn't you. Your heart is pure," Blake said. "That's why we need to get that memory out. The more darkness you have in your mind, the more the dark will take over."

"That's true," Adam said. "I struggle with this all the time. I cannot forget anything I read or see. When The Professor made me read those files about serial killers, they are now ingrained in my mind forever. I don't want that picture to be in your mind. I'm sorry Deanna pointed it out."

"It was an accident. I don't think she meant to hurt me," Holly said.

"She didn't," Adam confirmed. "She's just as horrified as the rest of us. We knew he was a monster, but we really didn't know the extent."

"Over there," Holly said, pointing with the hand Blake held.

Adam went over to the wall. He pushed on the tile Holly pointed out. It opened slightly. "Don't be afraid," Adam said. "Close your eyes if you need to."

"I can do this," Holly said clasping onto Blake's hand like a life preserver.

Adam opened the door. Inside was a metal box. He pulled it out and set it on the floor. "I need the key," Adam said, putting his hand out toward Holly.

Looking down, Holly realized she held keys around her neck on a necklace. "Where did these come from?"

"You hold the keys to your memories. Until you are ready to unlock them, they remain locked in your mind," Adam explained. "I need the key for this box. It's number 2591673."

Blake helped Holly look through the keys until they found the right one. Then Holly momentarily let Blake's hand go to release the key. She grabbed Blake's hand back and then handed the key to Adam.

Adam unlocked the box. Holly felt her heart rate pick up speed as he dug into the various pictures and files, unsure of what he would find.

"Here it is," he said, taking a picture out. "Blake, please verify this is the picture?"

Blake covered Holly's eyes. When Adam showed him the picture, Blake nodded. Blake kept an eye on Adam to watch how he did it. Adam took a lighter out of his pocket and lit the picture on fire. While it burned on the ground, Adam locked the box and placed it back into the wall. After closing the door, he returned the key to Holly.

Holly placed the key back on the necklace as she watched the picture burn. When it was ashes, the ashes swirled into the air until it was a clean floor once again.

"Do you still have the memory?" Adam asked.

"What memory?" Holly asked.

"Do you remember Deanna showing you a picture of your mom?"

"No. I showed her the picture of my mom's ID card. Her photo is not in the file."

Adam looked at Blake, who just nodded. "Okay. I need you

to close your eyes once again," Adam instructed. "Trust me. I'm not going to hurt you."

"I don't know why, but I trust you," Holly admitted.

"Because I've seen your heart. You are a good soul. You are not what The Professor said you were. You are kind. You are innocent of heart. The effect that picture had on you showed me all I needed to know. I've seen much in my short time of the darkness of life. The files I studied showed me just how dark this world can truly be. However, seeing the light in your heart shows me there is good outside of the walls of the campus."

"Thank you," Blake said appreciatively.

"She's my sister too," Adam said, taking her hand. "Okay. Close your eyes and take a deep breath."

When they did, they opened their eyes again to find themselves in the van. "You feel better?" Deanna asked.

"Yes. Why would I feel otherwise?" Holly asked.

Wyatt furrowed his brow. "You don't remember the picture?"

"Why does everyone keep asking me about a picture?" Holly asked. "If you're talking about my mother's, it's right here," she said, holding the ID up.

Baffled, Wyatt glanced from the road to the rearview mirror and back to the road again. "Is she serious?" Wyatt asked.

"The memory is gone," Adam said firmly.

"Completely," Blake confirmed.

"I don't –" Wyatt shook his head. Then he shrugged. "Okay. Anyone hungry?"

"Yes. Please?" Holly said. "I'm starving."

"That's a side effect," Adam commented, sliding all the pictures back into the folders, before handing them back to Blake.

"What is?" Holly asked, returning to the seat behind Deanna and Adam.

"When someone messes with your memory, you become ravishingly hungry. It's a tell," Adam explained. "We try not to do it too often. It's exhausting and a bit disturbing for the one doing it."

"Are you the only one who can do it?" Wyatt asked.

"No. Blake and Isabelle can as well," Adam said. "Blake now knows how. Isabelle and I have been doing it for a while. It takes a lot out of you."

"What can we eat?" Deanna asked, as Wyatt pulled into a restaurant.

Wyatt shrugged. "Whatever you want."

"What do you normally eat?" Blake asked.

"Only healthy, fresh foods," Adam said. "The Professor said he wanted our systems clean."

Holly pointed toward the shop at the gas station. "Can I get them something?"

"Take Deanna with you," Wyatt agreed. "The guys and I will go get a seat in the restaurant."

Once out of the van, Holly grabbed Deanna's wrist. "Come on," Holly said, excited.

"Holly? Your crutches?" Wyatt reminded her.

"No. I'm good." Holly waved him off. "I'm stronger than you think. With all that recovery time, I can do this. Those crutches make me clumsy."

"If you need them, do you promise to use them?" Wyatt asked.

"Yes," Holly agreed. Then she turned back to Deanna, "Come on!"

"Where are we going?" Deanna asked, running to stay caught up with Holly.

"Just come with me. Don't leave my side."

When they walked in, Holly made a beeline for the snack aisle.

Deanna shook her head. "I do not think this is Professor approved."

Holly grinned. "Exactly!"

Holly grabbed multiple candy bars, along with various snack bags. She stopped by the slushy machine, getting five slushies all the same flavor. The cashier rang her up and chuckled, "Going for a junk-food high?"

"Always!" Holly grinned, handing the cashier the money. "I'm teaching her the finer things in life."

"I don't know about the finer things in life," Deanna said, carrying one of the bags.

"Oh, honey. Bless your heart," Holly said and pulled out one of the slushies from the carrier. "Drink."

Deanna took the top off the straw and took a long draw. Holly saw the smile form on her face. "This is amazing! What is this?"

"That is a slushy. Now, try this," she said, handing Deanna a small chocolate bar.

"Oh my!" Deanna groaned in pleasure. "This is heavenly! What is this?"

"Chocolate. As women, it's our right to have some at certain times of the month. It's what stops us from killing guys during that time."

Deanna laughed, covering her mouth as she still had chocolate in her mouth.

"You have a pretty smile," Holly observed. "You should use it more often."

Swallowing the remaining chocolate, Deanna admitted, "I feel angry all of the time."

"I wouldn't doubt it. If I were under The Professor's thumb and getting thrown into that room all the time, I would be angry too."

"It wasn't fun."

"It will not be your future," Holly said. "I promise."

"How can you promise that?" Deanna asked. "You don't know him."

"I know you and Adam. I know you both know the truth. I

know you both know what our brothers and sisters can do and what we can do. I also know the more of them we free, the stronger we will all be. He cannot go against all of us. He will lose. He will pay for what he did to all of you and our mothers."

"I hope you're right," Deanna said, eating another bite of chocolate.

When she groaned in pleasure again, Holly laughed. Handing her another chocolate bar as they walked into the restaurant, Holly whispered, "Don't tell the guys you have this. They'll think I'm playing favorites. Us girls need to stick together." Spotting the guys, they headed over to the table and passed out the slushies. They enjoyed a wonderful meal of cheeseburgers, onion rings or fries, and chocolate bars for dinner.

DOUBLE TIME

"Change your thoughts and you change your world."
Norman Vincent Peale

*A*lex paced her office. Ben's shouts and rants played through her mind.

"Do not ever come near me or my family again. If I see you anywhere near them, there will be nothing on this planet that will be able to protect you!"

"You are a Judas. You wormed your way into our lives, knowing you were betraying us the entire time."

Tears streaked Alex's face. She did her best to control her emotions. However, whenever she thought she had them under control, another of Ben's shouts shot through her mind.

"It's your fault we're here. If anything happens to any of us, it will be on your conscience. Your choices have ramifications. I'm paying for mine right now. But you? You have to live with this mess you caused."

"I may be breaking your heart, but you shattered ours! Your father is killing us! I can only imagine what these rooms were used for in the past. Don't be naïve, Alex. Your dad is no saint! I wouldn't be surprised if he was related to Lucifer himself!"

"I'm so sorry, Ben," she whispered, hugging herself.

"Do not ever come back! Do you hear me? Don't come back!"

Alex looked toward the ceiling. "What do I do?"

"I said to leave! Go spend your money, Judas! Don't know the story? Look it up! You betrayed us all!"

Alex sat down at her desk and logged into her computer. Tapping away, she found the story on a site and clicked on the reference. Reading Luke 22:3-5, it said, *'Then Satan entered Judas, called Iscariot, one of the Twelve. And Judas went to the chief priests and the officers of the temple guard and discussed with them how he might betray Jesus. They were delighted and agreed to give him money. He consented, and watched for an opportunity to hand Jesus over to them when no crowd was present.'*

Alex rested her chin on her hand and huffed. "I haven't been infiltrated by Satan, but I see his point." She scanned the rest of the chapter, focusing on verses 47 and 48, *'While he was still speaking a crowd came up, and the man who was called Judas, one of the Twelve, was leading them. He approached Jesus to kiss him, but Jesus asked him, "Judas, are you betraying the Son of Man with a kiss?"*

"But I didn't betray Ben with a kiss. I truly love him." She sighed. "There's no way to fix this." Looking up at the ceiling she confessed, "I'm sorry for the part I played in this mess. Please help me figure out a way to make it right. I don't want to be the black queen. I want to be on the white side. I don't even care if I'm a pawn, as long as I'm on that side. I don't want to live in darkness anymore."

Just then, there was a knock on her door. Not even waiting for her response, The Professor barged into her office. "Alex, I need information!" he demanded, sitting in the chair opposite her at the desk.

Shoulders slouched, she said, "I'm sorry, Daddy. I don't have any answers. I failed."

"You did not fail, darling," The Professor said, sitting back in his seat. "You did your job for sixteen years. I just need you to see what information you can find out regarding where they are right now. We need to be ready. We need to be a team."

"Daddy, I don't feel like a team. I feel like I betrayed my friends," Alex admitted.

"Betrayed your friends?" His eyebrows rose in surprise. "Alex, they were never your friends. You have to know they knew who you were. That Sheriff dug deep. He knew you were with the clinic the entire time. I promise you he kept you on staff with the idea of keeping the devil he knew versus the one he did not."

She furrowed her brow. "What do you mean?"

Leaning forward, he asked, "Would you rather work with someone you know is your enemy or get rid of them, not sure who the enemy is?"

Alex thought about it for a few tense moments. "I guess keep the enemy I know."

"That's who you were to them."

"Wyatt trusted me. He even sent me on an assignment himself."

"Why?"

"What do you mean?"

"If he knew who you were, why would he send you?"

"Because he –" A smile formed on The Professor's face as a thought hit Alex. "He knew," she whispered in understanding. "He knew I would get rid of her ex-boyfriend."

"He knew exactly who was working for him. He knew how ruthless you were. After all, you are my daughter."

Alex dropped her head into her hands, shaking it. "How could I be so stupid?"

The Professor got up. Resting his hands on her shoulders as he stood behind her, he comforted her, "It's okay, sweetheart. I know who you are and love you just the way you are. I told you earlier you are a formidable young lady. I send you on assignments to protect us, this family. Wyatt sent you on an errand to do his dirty work. He didn't want to get his hands messy. He wanted you to do it for him."

Alex shook her head.

"You are my pride and joy," he said and kissed her head. "You are the light of my life. Your word carries the same weight around here, in this kingdom, as mine. You are a queen to them. In Willow Bend, you were a worker bee. You, my dear, were not as appreciated as you are here. Let me bring you back to our focus and goals?"

Alex sighed. Looking over her shoulder toward him, she asked, "Why can't I forget him? His words are echoing through my brain."

"He was your first love interest. However," he said, going back to his chair, "may I point out that he truly does not know you. He knew what you projected. You are like a chameleon. You blend very well into any situation. I don't know if you even know you're doing it. You, my dear, are an enigma. You probably don't even know who you truly are yourself." Leaning forward, he continued, "After this is all said and done, let's go down to the Bahamas for a few weeks to relax and unwind. Let's figure out who you are together."

Alex debated in her head for a few moments.

"Beach. Sun. Relaxation. No stress. Just daddy and daughter time. What do you think?"

"I think that sounds nice," Alex finally agreed. "Let's do it!"

"Brilliant!" He clapped his hands. "We just have to get through this tiny crisis, and it's rest and relaxation."

"I think it would be good for us."

"Agreed. Now, can you see what your people know? If they don't know anything, I need you to do your thing and go find them."

"I'll get right on that," she agreed.

"If that requires you to leave, let me know, and I'll give you the card. You can take a few of the guards with you to keep you safe."

"If I go, I'll go by myself. I move quicker without them."

The Professor nodded his head in appreciation. "Surgical."

"Yes. I'll tell you what. I'll go back down to Willow Bend and start there."

"That's fine. Just know if I need you, you'll have to get back to the private jet when I say. If Wyatt and company are coming, I'll need you here."

"Agreed. Just give me time to get to the airport. Which jet do I take?"

"Go ahead and take Javier's. Leave Marshall and his jet here with me."

"Sounds good. I'll take off in about an hour."

"Perfect! I'll let Javier know to gas up the jet," he said, standing. When he was almost to the door, he turned and added, "Don't let them deter you from the overall mission. They will try their best to mess with your head. Stay focused."

"Thanks, Daddy. You helped me refocus. I got this."

"Good girl," he said and left, closing the door behind him.

Alex sighed, dropping her head onto her crossed arms. "Now I'm even more confused than when this whole mess started." Glancing up at the computer screen, she saw the words of Luke 22:4-5 staring her right in the face, *'And Judas went to the chief priests and the officers of the temple guard and discussed with them how he might betray Jesus. They were delighted and agreed to give him money.'*

Looking toward the ceiling, she asked, "Which one do I listen to? Who do I betray? I feel like either way I look at this, I'm betraying either Ben, Wyatt, Hope, and the kids, or Daddy. In Willow Bend, it was pounded into my head that family is everything. How do I choose which family to show loyalty to? Which one do I honor? Have I already messed up everything with the Willow Bend family? What if Daddy's right? What if they knew the whole time and were using me to do their dirty work? On the flip-side, what if Daddy's been using me this entire time? Am I really a Judas? Am I the one betraying them, or are they betraying me?" She growled in frustration, slamming her fists onto the desk. "I need to get out here! I need space to figure this out!"

⟐⟐⟐⟐

"WHO KNEW THIS STUFF EVEN EXISTED?" Deanna said as they sat on the bed in their room at the hotel. Eating her candy bar, she closed her eyes as she chewed. "This is amazing!"

Holly giggled. "I think I may have created a monster."

"She hasn't even had a cookie yet," Blake said knowingly. "Imagine what she'll do with one of mom's fresh-baked chocolate chip cookies."

"More like a dozen," Holly said. "You can't eat just one."

"What do they taste like?" Deanna asked.

"May I?" Blake asked, walking over to the pair.

When Deanna nodded, Blake rested his hand on her arm. She closed her eyes as she saw in her mind Hope pulling a pan of chocolate chip cookies out of the oven. The smell was heavenly. Her mouth watered as she reached down and took one of the cookies Hope set on the plate.

"Be careful. The chocolate'll burn you," Holly warned.

Deanna smiled as she nibbled around the edge of the cookie in her mind. The cookie melted in her mouth. She blew on a chocolate area before biting into it. Groaning in pleasure, she opened her eyes to find herself sitting on the bed in the hotel once again. "I want one!" Deanna said. "Please?"

"I promise you Mom will make a party of chocolate delicacies that will blow your mind!" Holly winked. "She's an amazing cook. We'll have a huge party with everyone invited."

"Ya know, on cruise ships they have chocolate fountains. I've seen pictures," Blake said.

"Chocolate – what?" Deanna's eyes got wide. "Are you serious?"

"Yep! I think we'll need to have one of those at the party too," Blake said. "You can dip things in it like strawberries and pretzels."

"Definitely need one of those," Deanna agreed.

"Obviously, chocolate is the key to your heart," Adam said with a smile. Seeing Deanna smile made Adam happy. He had not seen her smile this much in a long time. He hoped with every bone in his body that Wyatt, Holly, and Blake were not lying. He hoped once this was all over, they could, in fact, live in this bliss they were experiencing permanently.

⊲◖⊲◖⊲◖⋔

"WE NEED to do something with these files," Tanya said to Colby. "We can't leave them here. I'm surprised they haven't raided us yet."

"Colby took out the SD card from his camera and replaced it with a new one. He continued to take pictures of everything he could. If they were going to possibly get raided, he did not want to lose all of this vital information.

When Ben took files, he took a lot. The files contained years of research, along with the schematics of the other buildings they were looking for, and the names of all of the subjects and carriers. Colby took multiple close-up photos of the schematics. If they had to duplicate them, he did not want to make a mistake. He marked each photo by layer before he took the close-ups of the floorplan.

By the time nine o'clock rolled around, the pair filled five SD cards. Colby took the SD cards and placed them in a sealed tube, before sliding the tube into his front pocket. He did not want anything to happen to the cards. When they replaced the boxes back in their place, they left the workshop and headed home.

"I wonder what –"

Colby slammed on the brakes of the truck, as Tanya was cut off by an explosion on the property. Wide-eyed, he asked, "We didn't do that, did we?"

"No. GO!" Tanya said, hitting his arm in a panic. "They know. You have the cards, right?"

"Yes. But I left my camera there."

"They probably thought the SD cards were there too. Go, Colby! Go!" she shoved his arm.

Seeing a car pull out of the driveway from down the road at high speed, Colby floored his truck. Tires spinning, spitting stones up into the air, he fishtailed before gaining control. Speeding toward the police station, they swung into the parking spot. Colby watched as the car sped past the police station. When the driver and Colby made eye contact with each other, Colby committed his face to memory.

"Do we go home?" Tanya asked.

Colby gulped. "I'm afraid we have to. Our parents will be scared to death. They haven't seen us all day."

"Don't say scared to death," Tanya said, taking deep breaths. "Let's not chance jinxing things."

"Good point. I have to tell you I'm scared. I'm really scared."

"I didn't think anything scared you besides spiders."

"Spiders don't scare me. They just creep me out. And, just because I'm big doesn't mean I don't get scared. These people are not ones we should be messing with. These people have had women killed and gotten away with it. They know more than they should. They seem to be a half-step ahead of us at every turn. I left my camera, but I have the SD cards. They were watching us, Tanya. They knew when we left. They probably went in right after to see what they could find."

"And when they found your camera, they thought they had all the pictures," Tanya finished his thought. "They were watching us all afternoon."

"I wonder what the others found, or if they ran into the same type of issue?"

Tanya pulled her phone out of her pocket and sent a group text. As the responses came through, Tanya read them, "Lindsey says she and Shawn had a difficult time connecting, but together they were able to find some information. She sent that to me privately. Shawn's response was they were fine."

"Of course he said that. Glad at least one of them is honest." Colby rolled his eyes. "What about Mac and Megan?"

"Mac and Megan both put they were okay and in Megan's basement. They said to come on over," Tanya read and looked up at Colby. "Do we do it? If we're being followed, do we want to put any of our friends or family in danger?"

"If we're being followed, chances are they are too, and our phones are tagged," Colby pointed out. "We're going to have to get together and figure out a way to meet without tipping our hand as to what we all have."

Tanya took Colby's hand into hers. "I'm going to ask a question, and I want an honest answer."

"Go ahead."

"Are we safe here? Do we need to leave? If so, do we all

need to leave? If that answer is yes, do our families need to leave?"

"That's more than one question."

"Do you have any answers?" Tanya asked.

"I think our families are safe," he said, giving her hand a gentle, encouraging squeeze before returning his hand to the steering wheel. "Our families don't know anything. It won't take them long to figure that out."

"Then, it won't take them long to realize we do know stuff."

"They already know," Colby said. Looking into the rearview mirror, he saw a car in the parking lot across the street from the police station. There were two men sitting in the front seat watching them.

⟨◊⟩⟨◊⟩

"ABOUT TIME you two showed up! Where have you been?" Lindsey scolded when Tanya and Colby walked down the stairs.

"We can't be here very long," Colby said. "None of us can."

"What do you mean?" Shawn asked.

"Remember your plan to go to a rodeo?" Tanya asked.

Shawn nodded. "Yeah."

"We may need to implement that plan."

"Why?" Shawn asked, uneasy.

"We were watched all afternoon," Tanya explained.

"And when we left, they decided to blow up Ben's workshop," Colby added.

"You're serious?" Megan asked, stunned.

"Very," Colby said, crossing his arms. "They also chased us to the police station, and then another set of their buddies decided to sit in the parking lot across from the police station and watched us until we left."

"Do we have everything we need?" Mac asked. "Do we have enough information to take to them?"

"That's not the question we should be asking," Megan said, turning around from her computer screen toward them. "We should be asking if our families are safe if we leave?"

"It doesn't sound like they're safe if we stay," Mac argued. "I don't think staying is an option. I wish there was some way to get ahold of the others so we can connect."

"If we leave, our families will be searching for us," Shawn said. "We have to do it so they won't worry."

"Is that possible?" Megan asked.

"Can we all get away?" Tanya asked. "Will our parents agree to us all leaving? It's not like we're eighteen."

Standing, Megan cleared her throat. When everyone looked up at her, she explained, "This is something we're going to have to do on our own. Mac, Shawn, and Colby can leave for a rodeo. Lindsey, Tanya, and I will have to figure out another outing to get us out of town. My parents will not let me knowingly leave town with boys and no adults."

Lindsey shook her head. "Mine neither."

"Mine would hunt me down and drag me back kicking and screaming, probably saying a string of words in Spanish I can't repeat," Tanya added.

"We need to come up with a plan," Megan said decisively.

"What if we just tell our parents we're heading to the rodeo, too?" Linsey asked. "I mean, they know we're friends. They also will know if we say it's a church thing since we all go to the same church. There's nothing on the schedule. We can tell them that we girls will room together, and the boys will have their own room on a different floor."

"The other alternative is to pretend like we're going to school, ditch school, and leave notes," Tanya suggested.

"What are they going to say?" Lindsey asked.

"What if we tell them the truth?" Megan suggested. "We could tell them we have stepped into something dangerous and don't want to put our families in danger. We could tell them we'll contact them when it is safe."

"They'll send out a national alert." Shawn rolled his eyes. "This isn't the eighties where we can get away with leaving without notice. With communication and tracking the way it is nowadays, it's difficult to disappear."

Tanya shrugged. "Then, we tell them we're going to the rodeo."

"Will they really let us go during a school week?" Megan asked.

"How often have you asked for time off during school days?" Mac asked her.

"Never."

"Make sure to point that out."

"Ooo! Good idea."

"I get those once in a while."

"So, if our parents refuse, then tomorrow morning, we meet before school and leave before school even starts?" Tanya asked.

"What vehicle will we take?" Mac asked. "None of the cars can hold all of us. There are six of us."

"What if we hotwire Ben's car?" Colby asked. "He has an old Caprice Classic. His car has two bench seats. It's also not known in most circles."

"No need to hotwire it," Shawn said. "Chances are, the keys are in their house. Mac and Colby can get the keys and drive the car."

"How can they get the keys if the keys are in Ben's house?" Megan asked. "Isn't it locked?"

"Colby is good at picking locks," Shawn said with a wink. "The best I've seen."

"I can do that," Colby agreed.

"I think that's a brilliant idea," Tanya said. "We can text to the group *rodeo* if we got our parent's permission, and *clinic* if we don't. We pack a bag with toiletry necessities, along with three changes of clothes each and something to wear to bed. We can wash clothes in the sinks of the hotels where we stay. I'll bring a bottle of laundry detergent."

"That sounds like a sound plan," Shawn agreed.

There were choruses of agreement from everyone else before they left for their perspective homes. Once they were gone, Megan went upstairs to her parents, who were watching the news.

"Y'all were out and about pretty late tonight," her mom mentioned, as she worked on a counted cross-stitch of Texas for a pillow to match the one already on the couch.

"Well, that's what I want to talk to you guys about if you don't mind?" Megan asked, sitting on the coffee table in front of them.

Her dad looked at her over his glasses. Seeing the seriousness on her face, he shut off the television. "We're all yours."

"Well, you guys know Mac and Shawn are rodeo riders, and usually Colby tags along with them to help, right?"

"Right," her dad said, uneasy.

"Well, the girls, meaning me, Tanya, and Lindsey are really curious about going to one. We've missed all those in this area and wanted to go to the one they have this week."

"Why can't you wait until next year?" her mom asked.

"We've all gotten a lot closer over the last few weeks. The girls have been going to the games to support Lindsey and the guys, and they have been coming to the UIL and art shows."

"That's really sweet of y'all," her mom said, still concentrating on her cross-stitch.

Megan let out a slow breath of air before she continued, "The guys have a rodeo in Wyoming this week. Lindsey, Tanya, and I want to go. The girls would be in a separate hotel from the guys, so there's no concern."

"I would actually feel better if you were in the same hotel as the guys," her dad countered. "If there is not going to be an adult present, I would rather the guys were able to look after you."

Her mom set the cross-stitch down and looked at Megan. "Are you asking to go on a trip with mixed sexes?"

"Mom, I'm seventeen years old. This is just one week. I'll call you when we get there, and each night if that's a stipulation?" Megan offered.

"She's going to be an adult next year, Brenna," her dad said to her mom. "If we don't start trusting her in our backyard, what will we do when she decides she wants to go on a cruise or to Europe after she turns eighteen?"

Her mom debated it in her head. "When would you leave?"

"Super early in the morning. They were thinking around five in the morning."

"You have school," her mom pointed out.

"I know. I have never asked anything like this before. Don't you trust me?"

"She's right," her dad stepped in to defend her.

"I get straight A's. I'm never in trouble. All I'm asking for is a week," Megan pleaded. "I'm asking for your trust in this."

Her mom considered it for a few more moments before she looked to Megan's dad and asked, "Scott?"

"I think it's a fair ask. I would rather she do it somewhat still under our guidelines and rules."

Her mom considered it a few more agonizing moments, almost too long for Megan's comfort. Finally, she nodded.

"You can go," her dad said. "Please let us know when you get there, along with the hotel and room number."

"Okay. Thank you," Megan said. She felt bad about lying, but she knew it was for their safety. If they thought she was in any danger, they would not let her go – even if it meant they would get hurt too.

After giving them each a kiss on the cheek, she ran upstairs to her room and started packing. Scooping up her phone from the bed before going to the bathroom to grab toiletries, she texted *rodeo*. She scanned the other responses. The guys all replied the same as Megan. Tanya and Lindsey did not reply yet.

Shoving her phone in her back pocket, she then grabbed various toiletries she would need. She tossed them onto the bed before grabbing a pair of shorts and an extra-large t-shirt to wear to bed. Afterward, she pulled three different outfits and tossed them onto the bed. She also grabbed six pairs of underclothes, along with six pairs of socks. While she understood the idea of three pairs of clothing, she would not negotiate when it came to socks and underclothes.

By the time she got her bag packed, Tanya had responded *rodeo*. Wondering if Lindsey would be the hang-up, she headed over to her window seat to do her journaling. While writing, she glanced outside and saw a car sitting slightly down the road. She pretended to write as she kept an eye on the vehicle.

When it was still there by ten-thirty, she picked up her phone to see if Lindsey texted yet. She clicked on the camera and blew it up so she could see the license plate and snapped the picture. She then pulled back a bit and took another of the car. They were not close enough for her to get the driver or passenger.

While she was on the phone, Lindsey texted *rodeo*. Megan was relieved to know they would have at least forty-eight hours, splitting the supposedly seventeen-hour drive via two days to travel toward Maine before they would be considered lost. While the trip to Wyoming would only be seventeen hours, the trip to the Rangeley Plantation area would be closer to thirty hours, making it at least a three-day drive.

Megan texted to the group: *school five – have visitors.* It did not take long for the others to confirm people were watching their houses as well. Knowing her parents were in bed, Megan shut off the light in her room, acting like she went to bed. The two people in the car remained in their vehicle, so Megan quietly made her way downstairs to the basement.

Once down there, using the streetlights to see, Megan tucked her five-terabyte drive into a bag, along with a computer she always kept off-line. She also grabbed the SD cards Colby and Tanya left with her. Putting everything, along with the papers Shawn and Lindsey brought over into the bag, she then secured it.

After that, she went over to the basement window. The people were no longer in the car. Megan's heart skipped a beat. She scanned the basement for somewhere to hide. Finding a small storage area under the stairs, she sat on the floor behind some boxes, out of sight of any possible light.

Heart racing, she prayed with every bone in her body for her and her parents to be safe. That's when she heard it. Above her in the living room, she heard footsteps. She wrapped her arms around the bag, clutching it close to her body.

She gulped. Her heart skipped a beat. "God, please keep us safe," she whispered, barely audible.

Hearing the first step onto the staircase, Megan held her breath. She tightened her arms around the bag. Hearing two sets of footsteps on the staircase, she closed her eyes, praying even harder.

A flashlight went by the wall of the staircase. She saw it through the cracks but did not move a muscle.

She heard them search her desk. Then she heard them move toward her bookshelves. Afterward, they started searching closets. Finally, she heard the door of the storage closet open. She thought for sure they would hear her heart pounding as the flashlight scanned the closet area.

"Did she leave already?" one man whispered.

"I didn't see anything. Did you?" another man whispered back.

"No. We need to find her. Have the others picked up the other kids?"

"Not yet. They're having trouble finding them too."

"These backwoods kids are smarter than we gave them credit for," the man growled. "Let's go. We have to find those kids!"

She heard them go up the stairs and across the living room. Only when she heard a car in the distance start, did she dare move. Slowly climbing out, she struggled to hear anything over her own heartbeat. She made her way out of the storage closet with the bag on her shoulder. She went over to the window to find the car gone. "Whew!" she breathed out. Dialing Tanya, she still listened for any noise in the house.

"Where are you?" Tanya answered the phone in a hushed whisper.

"Still at home. They just left."

"They left my house a little bit ago. When I saw them, I ducked out the back and have been keeping to the shadows. I'm near the school now."

"Have you gotten ahold of anyone else?"

"Colby and Mac are going to get Ben's car. Then they'll leave Colby's truck at the school before heading over to Willow's Bend Diner."

"The diner? Why the diner?"

"Public area."

"But it's closed."

"There's a truck stop across the street."

"Then, are we meeting at the truck stop or Willow's Bend?"

"Willow's Bend. We're meeting behind it. The guys will fill Ben's car and then meet us behind the diner. The cameras are toward the door, so stay to the side of the building."

"Okay."

"How long will it take for you to get there?"

"I don't have my bag. It's upstairs. I'm in the basement."

"Oh geez," Tanya groaned. "Okay. Is it safe for you to get back upstairs for your bag?"

"I have to. My cash and bankcard are upstairs. They're in my purse."

"I'll tell you what. I'll get ahold of Mac and have him and Colby meet you at the park down the road from you. Hide in the playset out of sight of anyone. You know what Ben's car looks like, right?"

"I don't think so. I only saw it when he dropped them off at church a few weeks ago."

"If it's the only car on the street, which it will be at this time of night, you should be able to recognize it."

"True."

"Text me the word *jungle* when you're on the way to the park."

"Will do," Megan said and hung up.

Silently as possible, she slinked up the stairs. Turning the handle of the door with a little pressure allowed for it to give without too much noise. Thankfully, her dad hates doors that creek, so they are all well-oiled.

Poking her head out the basement door, she used the streetlights to look around the house. Nothing seemed out of place. She looked out the front window to make sure the car was still gone, and it was. There were no new vehicles either, so she headed upstairs.

She knew where every creak was on the staircase. She had lived in the house since the day she was born. She would often sneak downstairs during Christmas to look at the presents when she was younger, so she quickly figured out where not to step.

Reaching the top, she went to her parent's room. Hearing her dad snoring, she headed to her own bedroom. Changing, she then grabbed her bag, purse, and cash and headed downstairs. Grateful they did not have an alarm system yet, she ducked out the backdoor of the house with barely a sound.

She texted *jungle* to Tanya as she made her way to the park, keeping to the shadows as much as possible. Once there, she tucked herself and her bags with her into the tall wooden playset at the park. Here, she could see from every direction. She was grateful Tanya knew what to do. At this point, Megan could not think straight.

◁◁◁◁◁▷

AFTER PICKING up Megan at the park, the trio headed to the truck stop across the street from the Willow's Bend Diner. "Wait here," Mac said, and used cash to pay for the gas before he filled the tank with as much as it would hold.

"Why did Tanya have us meet you at the park?" Colby asked. He sat in the passenger's seat while Megan sat in the middle of the front seat.

"Because I was still at home. Y'all seemed to be smarter than me and left your homes once you found out you were being watched," Megan replied.

"Don't be so hard on yourself. You had to get all the information. We only had to grab our bags."

"True. I'm just glad they didn't do anything to our families."

"It's not our families they want. They know we know about the clinic by now. They want to know what we know."

"I knew this was going to bite us in the behind." Megan groaned. "We should have gone with them. We could all be halfway to Maine by now."

"Oh, it's not going to take us long to catch up to them. We're all too much on edge to sleep. We're driving until we catch up with them."

"Do we know which way to go?" she asked.

"I sent an email to the account. They'll know we're on our way when they check it."

"I cannot imagine what they'll say."

"Doesn't matter. At this point, our lives are in danger. After we pick up Lindsey, Shawn, and Tanya, we're all going to empty our bank accounts, so we have cash. I have a feeling we're going to need it."

"Good. We'll have to stop at a few ATMs for me."

"Why?"

"Because I have two-thousand dollars cash in my savings account. As long as I leave twenty-five dollars, I'm good. The ATM will only let me pull five hundred at a time," Megan explained.

"This may be a matter where you pull the five hundred and then pull the rest from a bank in the morning."

"I can do that too. Do we have enough collectively to do this?"

"We have more than enough. We've all got plenty."

"Good. I have a feeling we're going to need it."

"I have a bigger feeling we're going to have to disguise ourselves," Colby said.

"What do you mean?"

"Our parents are expecting to see us in the morning before we leave. My truck is at school. The other vehicles are at the houses. When they get up, and we're not there, they'll worry."

"They'll send out AMBER Alerts before we're across the border," Megan said, wheels turning in her mind to figure out their options.

"Oh, we'll be across the border tonight," he assured her.

"What if we stop by a store open twenty-four hours and pick up scissors and hair color?"

"That and baseball caps for those of us with shorter hair."

"Sunglasses and regular glasses too. We need to not look like ourselves."

"Sounds like a plan," he agreed.

"Okay," Mac said, getting into the car. "Let's get the girls and Shawn, and get out of town."

"We need to find a store and get some things," Colby said.

"Like what?"

"Things that will help us not look like ourselves."

"What do you mean?"

"We need to get disguises," Megan explained. "Once the AMBER Alert goes out, it won't take them long if we look like ourselves.

Mac nodded in understanding as he pulled out of the parking lot into the diner parking lot. Once everyone loaded in, while he drove, Mac prayed for safety for all involved. He also prayed they would get everything in place before the alert went out so their families would be safe.

PRESSED FOR TIME

"Life is either a daring adventure or nothing at all." Helen Keller

$\mathcal{A}$lex landed in Tyler, Texas. From there, she would drive to Willow Bend. It would only take about an hour or so to get there. Once there, she secured a hotel room. Flopping on the bed, she let out a sigh of relief. "This feels like home."

As if he could hear her thoughts, Alex's phone rang. She groaned. It was The Professor. "Hi, Daddy!" she answered it, feigning being happy to hear from him.

"Hi, sweetheart! Are you landed yet?"

"Yes. I'm in the hotel. I'll start first thing in the morning. It's been a long day."

"What if that's too late?"

She sat straight up in her bed. "What do you mean?"

"Vince and Fred got over vigilant and blew up Ben's workshop."

"They did what?"

"They blew up his workshop."

"Um. Okay," Alex said as she got up and paced the room while they talked.

"Then they followed two of the teens. Those teens led them to the others."

"Okay. And?" Alex pressed.

"The men separated in an attempt to capture –"

"Why would they do that?" Alex asked, exasperated.

"Alex, darling, calm down."

"They are ruining everything! I can't get information from those teens if they're terrified!"

"I understand. You may want to see if you can find them. The men tried, but they cannot locate them."

"Where are the guys?" Alex demanded. "I need to go have a chat with them."

"They're at the hotel with you, down in rooms 315, 316, 317, and 318. Make sure they understand how displeased we both are with them."

"Oh! Trust me! There will be no mistaking that fact!"

"When you figure out where they are, leave two down there and bring the rest back."

"I will," Alex said. "Give me a day or so to see where they are. I want to talk to them. As far as they know, I'm a friend of the family."

"Play on that. Use their sense of compassion. Let them think you're looking for them too."

"Got it."

"Good girl," he encouraged. "I'm proud of you, Alex."

"Thank you," Alex said and hung up. "Of all the –" She stopped, mid-sentence, and sighed. "How am I supposed to find to them now?"

She left for the rooms of the guards. She knew she could not search for the teens that night, but she could find out what they knew and go from there.

◁◑◁◑◁◑◐

AFTER ALEX HAD a strong conversation with the men, she went back to her room, now more exhausted than ever. From what the men had told her, she would be surprised if the teens were still at their houses. She was pretty sure they ran.

"Great!" she said on a sigh as she dropped onto her bed. "Where do I go from here?"

She was tired, but she wanted to feel close to Ben. So, she got in her car and drove over to his house. Shaking her head at the police tape surrounding the workshop, she tucked her coat around her as she proceeded to the back of the house.

Picking the lock, she went in. She momentarily froze at the amount of dried blood on the floor. She remembered what Ben looked like. "What did they do to you?" she whispered.

She wandered into his room. On his nightstand was a photo of the two of them in a frame. She picked it up and hugged it to her chest. "I'll take this with me," she said, keeping it in her possession as she continued to wander.

She sniffed his cologne. She touched his pillow. She then made her way into Hope's room. The picture collage on the wall was of various outings they had over the years. Some had Hope, while others had Ben, but all had the kids in each picture. "I didn't mean to," Alex whispered. "I'm sorry, Hope. You look so happy."

Alex wandered into the kid's rooms. Kids. Blake and Holly were anything but kids. They had always been mature for their age. Looking at the photos around Holly's mirror, she had a smile on her face regarding some of the memories of cookouts, going to the county fair, going to rodeos, and going out as a group to the lake for a lake day. While there was no boat, they picnicked on the shore. They would also swim and swing on the tire, swing out into the lake and let go, dropping into the lake. Wherever the group went, they embraced life. She always felt a sense of joy and happiness with them.

When she headed into Blake's room, it was a different feel but still calm. The whole house had a calm effect on anyone who entered. *Well, almost anyone,* she thought, remembering the kitchen. While Holly's main room colors were purple, peach, and white, Blake's were navy blue, white, and tan. Both were nature kids. That was evident in the décor. She almost envied them the way they grew up.

Alex grew up in a world where her dad had power. Her room had a lot of pink and purple and looked like it could have belonged to royalty. Inside that room, she felt like a princess. Outside that room was a stark reminder of the real world in which she lived.

Standing in the doorway of the kitchen, clutching the photo, she took one last look around. "I love you, Ben. No matter what you think of me, you have of my heart. I will never let you go," she said, and left.

Returning to the hotel, she curled up on her bed looking at the photograph. "I really hope you make it through. I also hope you don't still hate me when you do."

"WHO ALL IS GOING IN?" Megan asked as they pulled into the store parking lot.

"Here." Mac put his baseball hat on Megan. "That will disguise you. You don't wear hats."

"Put on this hoodie." Tanya pulled a plain, gray hooded sweatshirt out of her bag and handed it to Mac. "You two go together."

"Are you sure?" Mac asked.

"Yes," Colby said. "I'll move to the driver's side and drive for a bit."

"Fair enough," Mac said, getting out. After slipping on the hooded sweatshirt, keeping the hood on his head, he put his hand out for Megan to help her out of the car. "Let's go."

As they walked in, Mac took Megan's hand into his. "For the cameras," he whispered.

She nodded in agreement as she accepted his hand. While they walked through the store, they picked up six travel mugs, all different colors. They also got some snacks for traveling. Then they landed in the health and beauty section.

"How are we going to disguise our hair color?" Megan asked. When Mac shrugged, she suggested, "What if we turn Lindsey's hair medium auburn." She picked up three medium auburn boxes since Lindsey had a lot of hair. She handed them to Mac for the cart. "I'm a redhead, so I'll turn mine black."

"That's a change!" Mac said, wide-eyed.

"We have to not look like ourselves. Who's next?" She scanned the colors. "Shawn is blond. We'll turn him into my twin," she said, tossing him another box of black hair color.

"Oh, he isn't going to like that one."

"Oh well." She shrugged. "He's not here to object. Colby's got brown hair. We'll turn him blond," she said, picking up a bleaching kit with toner. "If you think Shawn's going to hate me, check this out," she said, picking up another bleaching kit with toner. "We're going to heavily streak Tanya's hair with blond."

Mac could not help the laughter that escaped him. "You're telling her!"

"I don't have a problem with that. I'm turning mine jet black. She can't say anything." Turning toward Mac, she said, "Now it's your turn. You have dark brown. I'm giving you a choice."

"Let's go with blond streaks in mine," he said, picking up the box. "Who knows? I may like it."

"Let's do self-check," Megan suggested as they made their way toward check out. On the way, Megan picked up four different pairs of fake glasses, two pairs of sunglasses, a few different kinds of make-up, and make-up remover cloths. When Mac raised an eyebrow, she explained, "Disguises."

"Good idea," he said, avoiding the camera while they walked over to a check-out stand. "Make sure to have your back to the camera. Hand it to me, and I'll scan."

They checked out, both successfully not looking directly into any cameras. On their way out the doors, Mac asked, "How much are they going to hate us?"

"Probably a lot. However, we have to not look like ourselves. The girls are going to have to wear makeup, or in Lindsey's case, not wear makeup."

"What about us guys?"

"Sunglasses during the day, and with different hair colors, you guys should blend in okay. We also cannot go anywhere as a gigantic group. We can go in groups of two or three to throw off the AMBER Alert that will undoubtedly be sent out in a matter of hours."

"You think?" Mac asked. "Are they going to let them send it so early?"

"They may have to wait for twenty-four hours. Our parents may think we went earlier than planned."

"Then we need to get somewhere and get our hair colored."

"My thoughts exactly," Megan said as they climbed into the passenger side of the car. Handing the bags to the back, the others started going through them.

⊲▷⊲▷⊲▷

THEY DROVE for several more hours before stopping at a few banks in Arkansas for the ATM withdrawals. Once the banks opened in four or five hours, they would draw larger amounts.

They then stopped at a rest area to change their hair color afterward. Waiting in the bathrooms until the pre-agreed upon time, they washed each other's hair clean of the hair color before they looked in the mirror.

"Oh, my word!" Tanya exclaimed, looking in the mirror at her blond streaks. "This is wild!"

"I feel like I'm looking at a stranger," Lindsey said, running a brush through her curly auburn hair after drying it with a hand dryer.

"I wonder what the guys look like?" Megan asked, putting her hair up in a messy bun, pulling a few stragglers down to frame her face.

"Your black hair makes your blue eyes pop!" Lindsey exclaimed to Megan. "You look gorgeous!"

"I didn't think medium auburn would work for you," Megan said to Lindsey, "but it really does. You look Irish."

"And you," Lindsey said to Tanya, lightly picking up a few strands of her hair, "this is stunning!"

"Now for your least favorite news," Megan said to both Lindsey and Tanya.

Lindsey rolled her eyes. "What now?"

Handing her a make-up remover cloth, Megan explained, "Lindsey, you need to not wear makeup. However, you're going to love the fact that you get to help both Tanya and me with makeup."

"Really?" Lindsey squealed in excitement.

Tanya groaned. "Really?"

"Really," Megan said. "We're all yours, DaVinci. Do your thing."

Lindsey taught both Megan and Tanya how to apply makeup, as she did both of their make-up. "For me," she said, "I'm still going to wear a base, along with make-up that doesn't look like I'm wearing any."

"Nope." Megan shook her head to Tanya's laughter. "No

make-up at all. Even if you wear make-up that looks natural, it's your flaws that will disguise you. Plus, anyone who knows you at all knows what you look like with little make-up or your normal amount. There are photos of us on church overnighters out there. We need you with absolutely no make-up."

"I wouldn't be caught dead without –"

"You may get that wish if you put any make-up on," Megan cut her off. "There'll be an AMBER Alert put out any time. It'll have our descriptions and photos all over them. Since we've changed our coloring, we need to change our faces via make-up use as well. You do not get sunglasses either. Here," she said, handing Lindsey a pair of fake glasses she picked up at the store. "For you too," she said, handing Tanya a pair as well. "I sometimes wear glasses but no make-up, so this is my disguise."

"No fair!" Lindsey pouted.

"Would you rather have those guys find you?" Megan challenged.

"No," she said, dropping her head. "Let's go."

When they walked out, they were stunned to see the guys. With their hair colored, they looked so different. Shawn and Mac both cut their hair short. Shawn's was black, while Mac's had blond highlights, and Colby's was all blond. Colby and Mac also had glasses on. Shawn's hair was such a drastic change, he did not need anything else.

"You three look amazing!" Mac said, wide-eyed. "So different! Good different, but different."

"Incredible," Shawn agreed.

"Y'all look great!" Colby said, pleased. "No one will recognize us!"

"We need to get rid of our phones," Shawn said. When everyone looked at him, jaws dropped, he suggested, "Send one text to the parents, maybe a short conversation. After that, we have to ditch the phones. They're trackable. We can toss them into the trash at the rest area across the street."

"No phone at all?" Lindsey pouted.

"We can get a pay-by-use phone for emergencies. That way, no one can track it," Colby suggested.

"Okay. Next town with a store that has it, we'll get one," Megan said.

"Everyone, send a text," Shawn said. "Once we get a response from everyone, we can clear our phones. Once the phones are clear, I'll run across the highway and throw them away."

"Is it not too early?" Tanya asked. "Won't that wake everyone up?"

"It's five in the morning," Megan said. "Send it via Messenger. If they're up, they'll get it. If not, they'll get it when they wake up."

"Fair enough," Tanya agreed.

"We also have food in the car," Megan said, "Let's text in the car so we can eat while we wait."

After everyone got into the car, Megan passed out food, and they ate while they texted their families.

⟨▷⟨▷⟨▷⟨▷⟩

"WAKEY-WAKEY TIME." Wyatt walked into the hotel room with several plates of food stacked on a tray. He slept on the pull-out couch, while Deanna and Holly shared a bed, and Adam and Blake shared a bed.

Adam slowly sat up. "What do we get to try this morning?"

Wyatt grinned as he pulled off one of the lids. "Waffles!"

"Ooo!" Holly clapped. "I love waffles!"

"And mornings…apparently," Deanna mumbled, covering her head.

"I'm with ya, Deanna," Blake groaned, rolling out of bed before stumbling toward the bathroom.

"Wait until you try it," Wyatt said, holding out a plate.

Adam got up and got Holly and Deanna each a plate. Then he fixed one for himself while Wyatt fixed his own plate.

When Wyatt raised an eyebrow at Adam, he said, "Blake's on his own. I got the ladies their meal because they're ladies."

"Fair enough," Wyatt said and headed over to his bed to eat.

"Wow!" Deanna exclaimed after taking a bite.

"Try dipping it in syrup," Holly encouraged.

Deanna dipped a bite into the syrup. When she placed it in her mouth, she groaned in pleasure. "Oh! This is amazing!"

"This is just the beginning. You'll experience many wonderful treats in the future!" Holly grinned.

Deanna dropped her arm. "Okay. Now it feels like you're bribing me."

"No. I'm trying to show you there is more out there than what you knew in Maine."

"I'm sure there is," Deanna said. "It just feels unnatural."

"Living the way you were is unnatural," Blake mentioned, coming out of the bathroom. He made a beeline for the waffles and coffee.

"We don't know any other way," Adam said. "To us, it's normal."

"Well, hopefully this trip will show you a glimpse of how the real world operates outside of the world according to Professor Roth," Wyatt encouraged.

"Here's hoping!" Deanna said. "So, where are we heading today?"

"We're going through a part of Tennessee, Virginia, and Maryland, before we stay the night just over the Pennsylvania border," Wyatt explained. "Tomorrow, we're going to get just barely into Maine. I want to get to Rangeley during the daylight hours. At least make a plan during the daylight hours. We may do a day of recon first."

"That's smart," Adam said. "We can give you the lay of the land. As for an actual plan, that may take a little more time."

"We have two days to figure it out," Wyatt said confidently. "However, I learned long ago, most plans need to be fluid. Whatever the plan, it will inevitably get changed once in motion."

"We'll have to take your word for it," Adam said. "This is the first time we've been off the campus."

"The first time of many. Once we get all of you out of there, we'll get you back to Texas and settled into real life," Wyatt said. "Only then will you know what it feels like to be a real teenager. This mess you grew up in, void of real love, is not ideal."

"How long do you think it will take to get everyone?" Adam asked.

"That depends. But I give you my word that we will not stop until they are all out from under that man…one way or another," Wyatt promised.

"What does that mean?" Deanna asked.

"Whatever it takes, whether we make it out alive or not, we'll work together to get everyone we love out. That means all the kids, Hope, and Ben. All of them. That means I will put my life on the line if I have to."

"You would do that?" Deanna asked. "For real?"

"You were raised in a way no one should ever have to live. It's my mission to make sure you will live free for the rest of your life."

"That's a strong statement," Adam said.

"One I fully intend to fulfill," Wyatt promised.

"Me too," Holly said. "You guys should have been raised with us. You weren't. Whether we make it out or not, you need to know what real freedom feels like."

"Seriously?" Deanna asked. "What happens if you get killed?"

"Then, I'll fulfill their promise," Blake jumped in.

"I don't understand why though?" Deanna asked. "We tried to take you. We set your parents up to get taken back to that man. Why would you do this for us?"

"Deanna," Holly said, taking Deanna's hand into hers, "I'm not sure how many more times we can say this. You. Are. Our. Family. You give all that you are for family. We're in this together."

Deanna sighed. "All right."

"Hey, Wyatt?" Blake said, looking at his phone.

"Yeah?" Wyatt asked.

"We have an email from the gang. The clinic was hunting them down, so they ran. They're on their way to Maine."

Wyatt's jaw muscles tense, he demanded, "What did you say?"

"They started doing research," Blake explained. "They broke into teams. When Colby and Tanya left Dad's workshop after going through the boxes, the clinic guys blew it up."

"Wow," Holly said, eyes wide.

"They also broke into all of their houses, but they had a head's up and either hid or left," Blake said. "They all left last night in Dad's car."

"So, they're not far behind," Wyatt said in understanding. "Go ahead and send them this address. I'll reserve two more rooms. They need to sleep through at least one night if they're going to be any good to us."

"Any good to us?" Adam's eyebrows rose in surprise. "I can't believe you're even considering using them. That will put them in danger."

"They're already in danger," Wyatt argued. "I'm making a plan so we can keep an eye on them."

"What are we going to do with them when it's time to get everyone out?" Deanna asked.

"They may have to stay in a hotel until we get back," Wyatt said. "We'll make a plan. At this point, I would much rather they were with us than on the road by themselves. Email them the address."

"Yes, sir," Blake said and emailed them.

Wyatt crossed his arms. "Sit back and relax, folks. We have a long wait."

THE RIGHT TIME

"Only a life lived for others is a life worthwhile." Albert Einstein

"Got a text from my mom, as well as an email from Blake." Colby held up his phone. "They want us to meet them at this address."

"Give it to me, and I'll write it down. Just tell them we're on our way," Megan said, pulling out a notebook and pen from her computer bag. "Make sure you tell them we're ditching the phone too."

"Will do," Colby said, emailing them.

After gathering the information they needed from their phones, Megan and Tanya did factory resets on all of them. Then Shawn carefully made his way to the other side of the highway and threw them into the trash can. When he returned, they took off, stopping at a couple different banks once they opened to get more money from their accounts. Once they got the money, their next stop was the hotel where Wyatt and company were waiting for them.

◁◫◪◫▷

ALEX WOKE around ten the next morning. She went to each of the teen's homes. Seeing their vehicles in the driveway of those who had them, she knocked on the door of Tanya's home first around eleven that morning. When she told the parents who she was and that she saw all the kid's vehicles, she asked to speak with Tanya. When the parents did not find her in her room, calls went to the other parents. Scared, they all met at the school to see if they were there. That's where they found Colby's truck.

"They're gone," Alex said quietly to herself while the parents talked among themselves in the parking lot. "Smart kids."

The parents called the police. Alex ducked out during the chaos before the police arrived.

Heading back to the hotel, she got on the phone with her dad and shared what she knew. Once she was off, she thought through what she needed to do. She decided to leave the two nice guards in case anyone made it back. She did not want the guards making life difficult for them.

Getting on a plane within two hours of her call to her father, Alex felt like she was getting sent to prison. Resting her head against the back of the seat while the plane took off, she sighed. The guards were in the back half of the plane, while she in the front. She pulled the photo and frame from her bag. Lovingly running her fingers over Ben's strong jawline, lost in memories of the fun times they had together over the last sixteen years, she sighed.

"What am I going to do?" she whispered. "I feel I need to be loyal to Daddy, yet I feel a definite tug to Willow Bend...and you." She clutched the picture to her chest. "Ben," she whispered, looking up, "I know you're furious with me. Please don't give up on me. Please don't let me go."

⟨⟩⟨⟩⟨⟩⟨⟩

"THIS IS TAKING FOREVER!" Lindsey groaned, slumping back in her seat several hours later.

"We're driving across the country, not across town," Shawn snapped.

"Have you heard anything from them?" Tanya asked Colby, who had the burner phone they picked up two towns ago, along with an autonomous GPS.

"No. Pretty sure they're just waiting for us to get there," Colby said, checking it again. "How far out are we?"

Mac glanced at the GPS. "According to the GPS, we still have a few hours."

"What is –?" Lindsey was cut off by the phone in Colby's hand.

"AMBER alert," Colby said, pulling it up. He groaned. "They know we're missing."

"That fast?" Tanya asked.

"Someone must have messaged and not gotten a response," Megan said. "From that point, they could have tracked the phones to the rest area. Once they found the phones, it would be obvious we're not with them."

"Good thing we're already in disguise," Tanya said, looking out at the passing scenery. "I can't imagine what our families are going through."

"Remember why we're doing this," Shawn said. "It's for our families. Since the AMBER Alert went out, those Clinic people know we're not home. They'll leave our families alone."

"There's no way they'll get close to the families with the reporters crawling all over the place," Mac added. "Six missing teens will not go away anytime soon."

"How soon do you think they'll connect the Clinic to this mess?" Lindsey asked.

"If they check our searches on the computers, not long," Megan said. "But it'll take a bit to get to that. They won't find anything on my computer."

"You also have all the information," Tanya pointed out. "The Clinic people blew up the workshop with the evidence there. The only way they can connect it are through the library searches."

"That, or they'll do what Wyatt did, and check out Ben and Hope Hunt. That really won't take long," Colby said.

"True," Tanya agreed. "I wonder how Wyatt and the others are going to handle this?"

"We'll find out in a few hours," Mac said, tapping the GPS.

⟨⊕⟨⊕⟨⊕⟨⊕

"AW, MAN!" Wyatt groaned, looking at his phone.

"What's wrong?" Blake asked.

"There's an AMBER Alert for the kids," he said, holding up his phone.

"How are we going to handle that?" Holly asked.

"What's an AMBER Alert?" Deanna asked.

Taken aback for a moment, Holly took a deep breath before she explained, "An AMBER Alert is for missing kids. It was started back in the nineteen-nineties. I can't remember what the little girl's name was that started it."

"It was Amber Hagerman. She was abducted and brutally murdered in 1996. She lived in Arlington, Texas," Wyatt explained. "It was created as an early warning system to help find abducted or missing children. AMBER is also an acronym. It stands for America's Missing: Broadcast Emergency Response."

"I guess law enforcement knowledge base is vast," Adam said. "This shoots across the entire country?"

"It starts in the state the child, or in this case children, are from," Wyatt clarified. "If they feel they've crossed state lines, they'll move it forward to that state or the states they feel need to be appropriately notified. If it goes on too long, the other news networks around the various states will pick it up and broadcast it as well."

"I-I'm sorry for not knowing what it is," Deanna stammered, her face flushed.

"You wouldn't know what an AMBER Alert is because of how disconnected you were with the world," Blake said. "It's not your fault. There are a lot of things we're going to have to explain to y'all."

"We would appreciate it," Adam said.

"Please don't be afraid to ask if there's anything you don't understand," Wyatt said. "We don't think any less of y'all. We understand y'all were secluded up there in the clinic."

"Thank you," Adam said.

"I'm sorry. I do feel kind of stupid," Deanna admitted.

"You shouldn't," Holly said. "I'm sorry for my reaction. I just have to get used to explaining things. You are more intelligent in other areas."

"Such as?" Deanna asked.

"You're both extremely fit," Blake said. "You're not tainted by the world either."

"Well, I sort of am," Adam said. "Remember, I've studied serial killers."

"True. Deanna hasn't," Blake countered.

"True," Adam agreed.

"There's so much that'll be new to you," Holly said. "I'm excited to show you."

"We may have to slow that down for a bit," Wyatt said from his sofa bed. "With the AMBER Alert out on the other crew, we'll have to be careful how we proceed."

"True," Blake agreed. "I wonder if they know."

"They know," Wyatt said. "And I'm more than certain Professor Roth knows too."

⟨⟩⟨⟩

"DADDY," Alex said, knocking on the study door.

"Come in, love," he called out.

She walked in. Glancing around the room, she quietly made her way to the chair across from him and sat down.

"What is it?" he asked, not looking up from the file he had in front of him.

"First off, I'm back. I got in about ten minutes ago and came right over. Also, there's an AMBER Alert out for the Willow Bend teens."

"Do you know where they are?"

"That's a good question."

He glanced up at her. "One to which I expect you to find an answer."

"Daddy, it's a huge country! You cannot seriously expect me —"

"Alexandra," Professor Roth said sternly, interlacing his fingers in front of him as he looked pointedly at her.

Alex froze. She knew that tone all too well.

"You are perfectly capable of finding such a big group. One is a group of five, the other is a group of six. Are you seriously telling me with all of your connections, you cannot find eleven people, whom, I may add, are more than likely traveling together?"

She shifted uneasily in her chair. "It's difficult when they don't have their phones."

"They're teenagers." Professor Roth rolled his eyes. "What teen doesn't have their mobile?"

"They dumped their cell phones. That's what triggered the AMBER Alert after they figured out the kids left already."

"Alex?"

"Yes."

"No excuses. Find them!"

"Yes, sir," she said and left the study, closing the doors behind her. She finally let out the breath of air she held. "I have no idea how, but I will."

⟐⟐⟐⟐

Not hearing anyone for quite some time, Ben knew his time was limited. They could come at any minute. He shouted as loud as he could, "Hope!"

"Ben!" she shouted back.

"Hope, they'll be here soon. When they give you the medicine, think of the kids. Do not think of anything that scares you."

"This place is scary! It's terrifying everywhere I look!"

"I know," he said. Taking a few deep breaths, he noted how much harder it was to breathe lately. He knew his time was running out. The room was spinning. He struggled to make complete thoughts. He frequently saw things he knew were not there. "Close your eyes and think of Blake and Holly. Think of good memories when they come. I've been given this longer than you. I am not sure how much time I have left."

"Don't say that!"

"Hope, thank you for being by my side all these years."

"Ben?"

"You'll never know what the last sixteen years have meant to me."

"Ben! Stop it! We'll get out of this."

"I don't know if I'll make it. Too much poison."

"Will Wyatt and the kids make it in time?" Hope asked.

"I don't know. Please remember me when you pray?"

"Ben, I can't do it for you. You have to accept Jesus for yourself. Please take time to do that right now?"

"I won't do it just to save my soul."

"That's the only reason *to* do it! Jesus came to this earth to do just that."

"I would feel like a hypocrite."

"Get over yourself! If you don't make it out of here alive, you do know where you're going, right?"

"Where I deserve. I got you into this mess," Ben said, tears brimming his eyes. "If I didn't suggest taking Blake and Holly, we wouldn't be here right now."

"And, Blake and Holly would be instruments of destruction. What we did saved them. While I don't think God would approve of the method, I'm pretty sure He understands. What we did, we did for the better of those kids."

"I'm sorry, Hope. I wish things turned out better."

"Stop it, Ben!"

Just then, they heard the door at the end of the hall open, and both froze. Hope gulped as her heart raced.

Ch'clink!

Hope's door opened.

"Morning," Professor Roth came in with three large men. Showing her the phone with the AMBER Alert for the Willow Bend teens, he said, "Seems the children have found themselves in a bit of a predicament. I'll bet they're with Wyatt and the others. When they get found, they will all be arrested…or, do you want me to find them first?"

Hope narrowed her eyes at him. "I'll bet Wyatt finds *you* first."

"You think so? Have you not looked around lately? Armed guards are everywhere." He gestured dramatically, making sure to point out the four with him. "What makes you think they can even get within a hundred yards of this facility?"

"They're very resourceful."

"So are the children I sent for them. As a matter of fact, they are the strongest of my children."

"How do you know Blake and Holly aren't stronger?"

"Because my children were taught from when they were little how to defend themselves. They are tactical weapons themselves. They can be manipulative and conniving. I'll bet they somehow get Wyatt, Blake, and Holly to trust them."

"They're too smart for that."

"We'll just have to wait and see who's right. After all, Deanna and Adam were raised by me."

"You are a ruthless, callous, and manipulative, but the children in this facility have a mind of their own."

"Oh, no. They do not," Professor Roth taunted, throwing his head back in laughter. "I broke them years ago."

"They know what you are. They know just how cruel you really are. They know better than to listen to you once they're out of here."

Getting into her face, he sneered. "You may think that, but let me assure you they are more scared of me than of anything else on this planet. They will do what I say. They will bring Blake, Holly, and Wyatt straight to my front door with a pretty little bow on top. They will not fail me. They know better."

Hope stared into his cold eyes. There was not a hint of warmth anywhere in his soul. "You know you are not God, right."

"Yes. I am. I have created life. Therefore, I am a god. I have full control over my creations as well. I have also taken lives. Yes, I am in control of life itself. I am God!"

Hope burst out in laughter.

Professor Roth furrowed his brow. "What's wrong with you? Are you having a nervous breakdown?"

"You're God. You should know what's wrong with me," Hope shot. Then she got a grin on her face, as she said, "You are not God. You will never be God. There is only one Lord God Almighty. And while I do not wish Judgement Day on almost anyone, I will take a bit of pleasure when you stand before Him. When He sends you straight to Hell, I will wave as you go."

"That's not a very Christ-like attitude."

"Neither are killing innocent women, stealing their children, manipulating those children, and turning them into your own personal arsenal. Children are precious to the Lord. Have you ever picked up a Bible in your life?"

"Yes. I used to attend church as a youngster."

"Have you ever read Revelations?"

"I was taught various things as a child," he acknowledged.

"That's not what I asked. You see, if you actually read Revelations, you would know what's in store for you. I won't take revenge on anything going on here. I don't need to. The Lord will do that for me."

"You won't have the chance," he said, getting back into her face. "You only have days left on this planet. Your friend has hours."

Hope did not respond to him. It was useless. She closed her eyes. Taking deep, cleansing breaths, she followed Ben's instructions. She thought about the children. She remembered the kids running through the pumpkin patch when they were one. She focused on their smiles as the sun played with their hair. Their laughter and giggles echoed in her mind and she smiled.

Her next memory was when the kids were two. Holly spun the cupcakes around the kitchen, and Blake sat clapping in his highchair. The delight on their faces when they bit into the cupcake shot through her mind as they injected the amber fluid into her arm.

While the poison infused its way into her system, she focused on more of the various Sunday family outings they took. She remembered everything from the rodeos to the county fairs. She focused on the scents of the funnel cakes and cotton candy. She remembered the day Blake and Holly went to church with her. She focused on Pastor reading The Word. Despite the fears that attempted to penetrate her mind, she prayed and stayed focused on the good, using the only strength she had left... God's.

93

ALL IN GOOD TIME

"Life is made of ever so many partings welded together."
Charles Dickens

"They're here," Wyatt said, reading his phone as he stood up. "You stay here. I'm fixin' to check-in the girls. Afterward, we'll let the boys in the back door."

"Good idea," Blake said as Wyatt left, emailing Colby.

◁◁◁◁◁

"WYATT WANTS you three to check-in. Throw them off by being as ditsy as you can. You have to not be yourselves. If you want to pull some accent, go for it. As long as it's not southern, you should be fine," Colby said. "Once the girls are dropped off, we're to leave and then go park next to the back door. Wyatt'll let us in there."

"Sounds good," Megan said as she, Lindsey, and Tanya got out of the vehicle.

95

"Lose your southern twang," Lindsey said to Megan.

"Make sure to be as ditsy as normal," Megan shot back.

"Be nice, ladies," Colby said, before he got back into the car and they drove away.

"Lindsey, why don't you talk? I'll say stuff in Spanish. Do you know enough to interpret in case the person checking us in knows Spanish?" Tanya asked.

"Yes. I've been around your family more than enough times to pick up stuff. Your step-brother thinks he's smart speaking in Spanish at the games," Lindsey said, rolling her eyes. "I've interpreted when his remarks got crass."

"Really?" Tanya said, taken aback. "I guess I'll have to have a chat with him regarding respect when I get back."

"That is, if we aren't all tossed into juvie," Megan said on a sigh when they walked into the lobby.

Thankfully, Wyatt met them at the desk. At first, he raised an eyebrow at their looks and then cleared his throat before explaining to the desk clerk the extra rooms were for the girls. When Tanya said something in Spanish, Wyatt explained, "She wants to know if she can have extra towels?"

"Of course," the desk clerk said and left to retrieve a few extra towels.

"Good job speaking Spanish. That should throw them off," Wyatt whispered before the desk clerk returned.

"Here you go. Is there anything else I can help you with?" the desk clerk asked.

"Nope. Thank you kindly," Wyatt said. "Just the room keys. Thank you for getting the two rooms next to ours. We'll be checking out in the morning."

"Okay. Check out is by eleven."

"Oh, we'll be gone long before then," Wyatt assured him.

"As you know, breakfast is from six-thirty to nine."

"Understood. C'mon, ladies. The others are anxious to see

y'all. Glad you could make it," Wyatt said, ushering the girls down the hall.

Tanya said something in Spanish to Wyatt.

As they were going out of earshot, Wyatt responded to Tanya's question loud enough for the desk clerk to hear, "I'm sure she'll be excited to see her cousin after so long. We can hook up with the rest of the family in a bit."

Once they reached Wyatt's room, he directed them to the room connected to theirs. "Just open the adjoining door. I'll have them open our door as well. I still have to bring the boys in. You guys look different. Great job with the disguises. I wouldn't have recognized you if I didn't know you so well."

"Thank you," Lindsey said, using the keycard to get into the room.

Poking his head in his room, Wyatt instructed Blake to open the adjoining door before he ran to the back door of the hotel.

"Hello, ladies," Blake said, opening the door between the rooms. The girls already had their door open.

Tanya ran to Blake, throwing her arms around his neck. "I'm so glad to see you! You have no idea what we've been through!"

"You're shaking," Blake said. He took a moment to wash over her with calmness. He calmed the other two as well. Picking up strands of her hair, he mentioned, "Looks different."

"Do you like it?" Tanya asked.

"Of course I like it. You look good in just about anything."

"What happened?" Holly asked, as Megan and Lindsey walked into their room. "Whoa! Y'all look way different!"

"I know. We had to in order to mess with the AMBER Alert information. There's a lot that happened, but the big one is the Clinic people blew up Ben's workshop just as Colby and I left," Tanya explained.

"They also broke into all of our houses to find us and try to find out what we knew," Megan added. "We saw them just in time."

"Before we saw them, though, we had to convince our families to let us go to Wyoming for a rodeo," Lindsey jumped in. "At least that's where they thought we were going. They figured out something was wrong a little bit ago. Our guess is they tracked our cell phones, despite them being off and reset, and found them in the trash at the rest stop."

"Didn't y'all pull the batteries?" Blake asked.

"You can't pull a battery from an iPhone," Lindsey explained. "We turned them off and cleared the phones, but that was the best we could do."

Wyatt walked into the room with Mac, Shawn, and Colby. When he did, Holly jumped up and ran over to Colby, wrapping her arms around him. "I'm so glad you are all safe!" she said.

"I'm not sure how safe we are," Colby countered, wrapping his arms around her. "We're kind of caught between a rock and a hard place, and both are owned by the Clinic. They hunted us down in Willow Bend, so we ran to save our families."

"With the AMBER Alert, they'll leave your families alone," Wyatt said confidently. "It's you they want, not them. They know you're gone."

"Unfortunately, they probably have a good idea of where we're headed," Shawn pointed out.

"So much for a surprise attack, but we'd rather have y'all safe." Wyatt sat on his bed while the others found places to sit. He then continued, "We're going to have to get y'all landed in a hotel until we finish in Rangeley."

"We don't have a problem with that," Mac said. "We understand we won't be of any help, but actually a hindrance. Y'all can't be worried about us. However, on a good note, we bring gifts." He gestured toward Megan.

"Incredible how just changing your hair color and a pair of glasses changes the way you look," Holly said, ruffling her fingers through Colby's now blond hair.

Megan left the main room and grabbed her bag from her bed.

When she returned, she pulled out her computer and explained, "This computer is permanently offline. There's no tracking this one. I use it for things like this." As the computer booted up, she handed Wyatt the papers. While he skimmed over them, she explained, "Tanya and Colby got photos of all of Ben's files he left in the workshop before it blew, including the schematics of all three campuses. Meanwhile, those papers are articles Lindsey and Shawn found on microfiche about your precious Professor Roth. And, this handy-dandy terabyte drive contains what I found on the dark web about the facility, the others, and Professor Roth," she said, holding it up.

"You guys did your homework! Well done!" Wyatt said, impressed.

"Thank you!" Adam grinned. "I'm so glad you found the other sites."

"Yes," Megan confirmed. "Tanya and Colby found them in Ben's research."

"One's in Wyoming, south of Creston, and the other is near Corbett, Oregon. Both are in the middle of nowhere," Tanya explained. "However, Colby thought to take pictures of them, and Megan has all the SD cards full of the pictures."

"Wonderful!" Wyatt's face lit up. "That'll save us a lot of work!"

"That's also what got us into trouble," Tanya added. "They were watching us."

"They also followed us to the Police Station before following us to Megan's," Colby added. "They weren't overly subtle about it either. I'll never forget the face of that man following us from Ben's house. Pretty sure I could ID him in a lineup. The look on his face told me all I needed to know about him."

"This picture tells me all I need to know about this man," Lindsey said, holding up a photograph of Professor Roth.

Tanya shuddered. "Those eyes."

"They are not kind," Deanna admitted.

"He's a sadist," Adam added, "and a serial killer."

Lindsey's jaw dropped. "A serial killer?"

"He killed the mothers of all who have the gene," Deanna explained.

"Seriously? Do you realize how many of you there are?" Colby asked.

"Not really." Adam shook his head. "We just know there are more."

"Try twenty-six total," Megan said. "There were nine in Maine. The Oregon site is the next one with nine. And the Wyoming site has eight with the youngest group. The kids were named by the letters of the alphabet, and each group was born within a month of each other."

"Well, ours are me, Blake, Charlie, Deanna, Eddie, Freya, Gemma, and Isabelle," Adam said. "What are the others?"

"Let me see," Megan said, looking at the names. "The Oregon site has: Justin, Kelsey, Lexi, Mitchell, Nicholas, Owen, Piper, Quinn, and Ryder. They're all thirteen years old. The Wyoming site has: Sydney, Tessa, Ulyssa, Vince, Willow, Xander, Yvette, and Zoey. That group is ten years old. All the groups are three years apart. He probably stopped until he could get this generation through to help the next generation."

"Okay," Wyatt jumped back into the conversation, "I have a problem I've been struggling with since y'all contacted me."

"What's that?" Shawn asked.

"Y'all are okay, but your families don't know that," Wyatt said. "As a Sherriff and the designated adult here, I feel the need to call them so they won't be worried sick. I'll tell them to keep the AMBER Alert going and act as if y'all are not found, but let them know I'll keep you safe until we can get back."

"I would feel better," Megan said. "I felt horrible lying to them."

"I know, but it was for their safety," Tanya said. Turning to Wyatt, she asked, "Can you contact them and the Clinic not know about it? Do you think they'll be able to keep acting as if we're still lost? We want to keep them safe."

"Yes," Wyatt said. "I'll tell your parents only, using the burner phone, and make sure they don't tell your brothers or sisters. They need to keep acting as if you're still lost."

"I would feel better too," Mac said. "They don't deserve this, but we want to keep them safe."

"I can do that. Let me go to the other room to call," Wyatt said and left for the girl's room.

While he was gone, the others went over the information the teens brought with them.

"This is incredible!" Blake said, looking at the schematics several minutes later. "This will help us out a lot!"

"You do know you cannot go in with us," Deanna said to the Willow Bend teens.

"We do," Colby agreed. "Unfortunately, we can't go home either."

"As Wyatt said, we'll get you set up in a hotel and swing by to pick you up when we head to the next group," Holly explained. "We know at any point in time, they can use you guys like they're using Mom and Dad."

"And that's not a good thing," Blake said. "Our minds will be divided. Once we rescue the teens from Maine, along with Mom and Dad, we'll get everyone settled and then head over to the next one."

"How many are we taking with us?" Deanna asked.

"Honestly?" Blake asked. "Probably just the strongest. The others can look after this bunch and keep them safe."

"As long as we get them all, I don't care how we do it," Adam said, reading the articles. "The more I learn about that man, the more I personally want to take him out."

"He needs to pay for his crimes," Holly insisted.

"Hello?" Deanna said sarcastically. "Do you not know who you're talking about? If he's not dead, he'll come after us. He killed at least twenty-six women that we know of, maybe more. He's not spent one day in jail for it either."

Tanya gasped as a thought hit her. "Do you guys know who Alex is?"

"Alex who?" Adam asked.

Megan held up a photograph of Alexandra Murphy.

Adam shook his head as he passed the photo to Deanna. "No idea."

"Nope," Deanna said. "Never saw her before."

"Wait a minute. Let me see that," Adam said, putting his hand out for the photo. When he got a good look at it, he cocked his head to the side. "I've seen this girl's picture before, but she was a lot younger."

"Alex has been in Willow Bend for almost sixteen years," Blake explained. "That's a lot of time to change. She's been working for Wyatt. Are you sure it's the same girl?"

Adam thought for a moment as he closed his eyes, searching his memory. When it hit him, his eyes flew open. "She was younger. It's a picture of Professor Roth's daughter. He has it on his desk."

"Professor Roth's what?" Tanya asked, stunned. "She's been in Willow Bend this whole time!"

"I'll bet she was reporting back to him," Deanna said.

"She disappeared right after Mom and Dad were taken," Blake added.

"Because her job was done," Adam explained. "Chances are, she's up in Maine."

"Who is?" Wyatt asked, coming back into the room with a smashed phone in his hand. He tossed it into the trash can before sitting back down on his bed.

"Alex is Professor Roth's daughter," Blake told him.

"Are you serious?" Wyatt asked, color draining from his face. "Are you sure?"

"Yes," Adam said. "There's a picture of a younger version of her on his desk. I'm sure of it."

Wyatt dropped his head in his hand, shaking it. "It makes sense. I should have trusted my instincts and fired her a long time ago."

"She would have figured out how to weasel her way in anyway. Don't beat yourself up." Deanna waved him off. "Look who her father is. She's probably just like him."

"I'm sorry, guys. This whole mess is probably my fault."

"It's not your fault, Wyatt," Holly encouraged. "Professor Roth is the only one to blame for this mess. Now, what's the plan?"

"I contacted all of your parents. I talked to one of each and explained the situation. They agreed to keep it from your siblings, along with the news and social media. They'll act as if you're still lost. In the meantime, when we travel through Philadelphia, I'm fixin' to get you six set up in a hotel." He pointed to the Willow Bend teens. "You'll stay in the rooms. I'll get you adjoining, so you can keep an eye on each other. Please don't make me regret it."

"You won't. There are no relationships amongst us six," Megan assured him.

"Good. You'll order from room service only. No delivery. I'll take care of everything. Understand?"

"Yes, sir," Shawn said.

"When we rescue everyone else, we'll come through and pick y'all up. Since we still have to get to Oregon and Wyoming, I want to have you all a little closer to Texas in case something goes wrong. We may drop you off in Dallas, so when we go home, we can bring you with us."

"Shouldn't we be closer to you all in case you need us to help in some way?" Megan asked.

"It's a thought. Let's see how this goes," Wyatt debated. "Once we're done with Maine, I'm hoping the others'll be easier.

I'll also get another fifteen-passenger van for you guys. With the number of kids we'll have, we'll need the room. Ben can probably drive his car, and Hope can drive the van."

"You do know Hope and Ben are probably not in good shape right now, right?" Deanna asked. "Professor Roth is a heartless man."

"I can't imagine what he's doing to them," Adam said somberly. "I'm sorry for the part we played in this."

Holly shook her head. "You didn't know."

Adam apologized again. "We're still sorry."

"Okay. We need to take off in the morning. I want you guys to have a good night's sleep," Wyatt said to the teens.

"Wyatt, while we appreciate the idea of sleep, I have a feeling Hope and Ben's situation is time-sensitive," Megan said. "We'll have plenty of time to sleep in the hotel."

"What are you saying?" Wyatt asked.

"I'm saying I have a feeling this is a race against time."

"It's not the length of life, but the depth of life." Ralph Waldo Emerson

lex snuck down to the basement in the middle of the night. She got a key from one of the security guards for the isolation rooms. Knowing which room Ben was in, she unlocked his door and walked in.

"Alex?" He squinted his eyes to see better. "Is that really you or another nightmare?"

"Nightmare?" She gasped as she brought her fingers to her lips. "You consider me a nightmare?"

"You are my worst nightmare. Even worse than this poison in me."

"You can't mean that."

"Ha!" He laughed. "You spied on our family for years! You fed us to the wolves. How is that not a nightmare?"

"I-I'm sorry."

"Yes. You are."

"I-I need to ask you something."

Ben huffed. "You don't have the right to ask me anything."

"Please?"

"What?" he snapped. "What does the high and mighty princess desire?"

"Ben, please stop."

"No. You stop! You're acting like this came out of nowhere! You were spying on our family! We loved you! *I* loved you! How am I supposed to react to you? You betrayed us."

"I-I know I don't deserve it, but I came to ask you to forgive me?"

Ben laughed even louder. "Wow! You have some nerve! We welcomed you into our family with open arms. You not only made sure to spy on us, but also set me and possibly Hope to be killed. I'm not making it out of here. I promise you. I know what my body feels like. It's mush inside, Alex. My insides are pretty much melting. I have blood coming out of places where it shouldn't be. I'm seeing things. I'm hearing things. I'm not good. This is all being done because of you and your father. And you have the nerve to ask me to forgive you?" He laughed again. "Wow. Just wow!"

"Ben," she crouched in front of him, "I really do love you."

"Then cut me and Hope loose and get us to a hospital!" he growled. "What part of *we're dying* do you not understand? That man is killing us! Your father is literally killing us!"

"Wyatt and all of the kids are on their way. I just need you to hold on for a little bit longer. I wish I could do more."

"*Wish* you could do more? You're the high and mighty princess of this complex! When you told me who you were, I was stunned. I knew of Princess Alex, but I didn't recognize you in Willow Bend. You made us like you. I fell in love with you. However, I know you're his daughter now. There's no getting around what an evil, vile, poisonous snake you are!"

"Ben." She stood, shaking her head. "I'm so sorry! Please? I'm not a Judas."

A smile slowly formed on his face. "You read the story?"

"Yes."

He wiggled his eyebrows. "What are you getting in exchange for spying on us and turning us in?"

"Nothing. He made me do it."

"You're not getting a reward of any kind?"

"No."

"After this is all over, there's absolutely no reward coming your way?" he challenged. "You forget, I know your father. Don't lie to me!"

"H-he said we were going to go on vacation, but that's not a reward."

"Where are you going?"

"The Bahamas," she admitted.

His eyebrows rose in surprise. He started to laugh, but the blood caught in his throat, so he broke out into a coughing fit. Once he got it under control, he cleared his throat and looked pointedly at Alex. "You're not an idiot, Alex. Are you honestly going to tell me that going to the Bahamas is not a reward?"

"It's supposed to be family time."

"It's bribery. It's a reward for being a good little girl and obeying daddy," Ben countered. "He's got you so twisted up that you have no idea what he's doing to you! He is the master manipulator. How do you think this will ultimately turn out?"

"I –" She shook her head. "I don't know how to answer that."

"He's manipulated you all of your life. You just keep doing what daddy wants, and you will keep getting rewards. If you start to stray, he bribes you or comes up with some type of crisis he knows you can handle to bring you back into the fold." He sighed, shaking his head. "Alex, I have to ask you something, and I want you to think clearly when I ask. Which life did you like better? The one here or down in Willow Bend?"

Without hesitation, she responded, "Willow Bend."

"That's because you were out from under his thumb. He keeps you on a leash, ready to pull you back whenever he needs you. He left you in Willow Bend, because he kept getting information from you. You were useful to him. As long as you are of use to him, he'll keep you around." Seeing the tears crawl down her cheeks, Ben let out a slow breath of air as he tried to calm the anger that wanted to explode like a volcano. "Look. I liked you. I was even in love with you. I'm not going to deny it. I had no idea you were the spawn of the devil, though."

Alex took a step back, shaking her head as she covered her mouth with her hand. "No. I'm not like –"

"What you did to our family…to me…you have to live with for the rest of your life," he cut her off. "Take a good look at me, Alex. This is your fault!"

"I-I'm sorry. I didn't know he would do this to you."

"What did you think he was going to do? Send us to the Bahamas? This is who your father really is. He's not that charismatic, charming Englishman the nurses around here seem to fawn over. No!" he shouted, and she jumped. "He's a ruthless killer. He's a barbaric crime against humanity! That's who your father is!"

"That's-that's not who I am, though," Alex defended herself.

"Who are you, Alex?" Ben narrowed his eyes. "Who really is Alexandra Murphy? Are you the fun-loving, sweet, sometimes awkward girl you were down in Willow Bend? Or are you the spawn of Satan? The manipulative princess of this horrendous, twisted kingdom. Which Alex are you?"

"I don't care if you don't believe me! I'm the Alex you knew in Willow Bend!"

"Prove it! Release us!"

"I can't," she admitted, looking down. "We would get killed trying to get out of here. Daddy has extra guards on duty in case Wyatt comes in guns blazing."

"I hope he does! Take notes, Alex. That's how you should be reacting when someone takes your love!"

"I just –" She shook her head and went to leave.

"Stop," Ben said. When she turned around, he got a good look at her. He saw the struggle in her eyes, and ultimately in her heart. "Alex, I'm doing this as much for you as I am for me. I forgive you. However, do not, and I mean it, do not come back down here again. Your conscience is clear. Leave and never come back. If you do, I will not forgive you again."

"Thank you," she said, practically a whisper. "I do love you."

With that, she left, locking the door behind her. After she returned the keys to security, she went to her room and cried herself to sleep. It was not a rest-filled sleep by any stretch of the imagination. Her soul was in a battle between pure evil and goodness.

❖❖❖

AFTER SETTLING the rest of the teens into a hotel in Philadelphia, Wyatt, Blake, Holly, Deanna, and Adam raced for Maine. Knowing their time was limited in saving Hope and Ben, they did not want to waste any more time.

As they lay in bed in their hotel in Maine, none were sleepy. They were on edge.

"Wyatt, can we do this?" Blake asked.

"Yes. We can," Wyatt said. "With God on our side, we can do this."

"If we don't, Hope and Ben don't have a prayer," Holly said.

"I don't know about this God of yours," Adam said, "but I do know how strong the four of us are together."

"I wouldn't want to go against the four of us," Blake said in a chuckle.

"I agree," Wyatt said. "I'm glad y'all are on our side!"

"We will get to them," Deanna said. "I only hope it isn't too late."

⟨⟩⟨⟩⟨⟩⟨⟩

HOPE HAD three doses of the amber fluid. She cringed every time she heard the door unlock, thinking they were bringing more. Ben did not sound healthy the few times he tried to talk to her. Knowing what he sounded like and what she felt, she was not sure he would make it out of this alive.

"Ben?" Hope called out.

"What?" Ben yelled back. When he yelled, it strained his throat and he started coughing. "Hope!"

"What is it?" she asked, hearing an urgency in his voice.

"I've coughing up blood. It's bright red now. I'm getting worse."

"I saw the syringe. They're only giving us 1 cc of the amber fluid. You shouldn't be this sick this fast."

"Yes, but I've had several doses. I don't –" He was cut off by another coughing fit. "This isn't good. I feel…there's blood everywhere, and my insides feel like mush."

"Do you know what it is?" Hope asked.

After he slowed his coughing, he admitted, "I'm not sure, but I have my suspicions. I think there's more than what we think in that syringe. We're at their mercy."

"Ben, I want to say some things to you, but I don't want you to interrupt. I just want you to listen and consider what I have to say. Will you do that?"

"For you? Of course."

"I first want to say thank you for giving me the wonderful gift of those two amazing children and the honor of raising them with you. You'll make an incredible husband to a fortunate young lady someday."

"Not at the rate I'm going. I'm going to be honest. I don't think we're getting out of this."

"Ben, please just listen."

"Okay," he relented.

"While you are a great man, my bigger concern is for your heart and soul. You know I'm a Christian. You know I gave my life to Christ long ago and have been His servant. I also know you have not. While it is not my place to judge your heart, knowing you as well as I do, I highly doubt it."

"Hope, I –"

"Please just listen for a few?"

"Go ahead."

"Thank you," Hope said, relieved he was not going to argue. "As much as we love our kids, God loves you more. Jesus even gave His life for you, just so you could experience Heaven with eternal peace when you die. Life has enough ups and downs. There are times where living here on earth can be terrible. However, I promise you it's nothing like you will experience when you go to literal Hell."

"I appreciate what you're trying to –"

"You told me you would listen," Hope scolded.

"You're right. I'm sorry. Go ahead. If we don't make it out of this, I don't want you yelling at me in the afterlife."

"That's the thing," Hope said. She took a breath of air and slowly let it out. Saying a prayer in her head for clarity, she continued, "John 5:24 says, *'Very truly I tell you, whoever hears My word and believes in Him who sent Me has eternal life and will not be judged, but has crossed over from death to life.'* If you die and have not given your life to Jesus, you will be judged and sent to Hell. John 11:25 says, *'Jesus said to her, "I am the resurrection and the life. The one who believes in Me will live, even though they die."* We're all going to die, Ben, just as we were all born. Those are the only true guarantees in this life. I pray you make the right choice before you go."

"Aren't you scared?"

"I'm more scared of how I'm going to die than actually dying," Hope admitted. "Matthew 10:28 says, *'Do not be afraid of those who kill the body but cannot kill the soul. Rather, be afraid of the One who can destroy both soul and body in Hell.'* Right now, that is who you are following."

"I'm not following anyone right now."

"You are. If you do not choose to follow Jesus, then you are automatically one of Satan's. John 3:18 says, *'Whoever believes in him is not condemned, but whoever does not believe stands condemned already because they have not believed in the name of God's one and only Son.'* Satan knows he's lost, and when Jesus comes back, Satan's time is up. He also knows he cannot touch the soul of a Christian. Once we are a child of God's, Satan can only hurt us from the outside...and only if we give him permission by not resisting. However, if he can distract you long enough for you to die without accepting Jesus, then he has you to torture for all eternity."

"Hope, you need to understand something."

"What?"

"I used to be a Christian. I used to be a leader in youth group and in High School for Christ. I event went to a Bible college."

"What happened?"

"When —" he was cut off by a coughing fit. When finished, he spit blood onto the floor before he continued, "When I was in High School, my family adopted a young girl named Joey. She came out of a severely abusive situation. She came to live with us Christmas Eve one year. We were able to adopt her a year later. And, about a month after we adopted her, she finally accepted Christ as her Savior."

"That sounds great!"

"Now it's your turn to listen, Hope."

"Fair enough. Go ahead."

"Several years later, she and I came home for college break.

At the time we got home, the rest of the family were at the Christmas pageant at church. They were supposed to be home any time. When we got out of the car, a shot rang out, and I dropped to the ground with a searing pain in my leg. Joey ran to my side. When she was almost to me, her birth father stepped out of the shadows and shot her in the chest. She dropped on the ground right next to me."

Hope gasped. "I'm so sorry!"

"Hope?"

"Go ahead."

Tears poured down his cheeks as the memories flooded his mind. "As soon as he shot her, he ran. That's the only thing I was thankful for that night. My family pulled in five minutes after he left. That was the longest five minutes of my life. I had to hold her while she died in my arms, and my leg was bleeding."

"What happened next?" Hope asked.

"As her soul left her body, my family pulled in. I didn't cry. I was angry."

"I would be too!"

"You don't understand how angry I was. Furious didn't cover it! Mom and Dad called the police and ambulance, but it was too late. I struggled. I fell hard. I spiraled. I couldn't understand. I lived, but she didn't. I couldn't protect her. The courts failed her by letting that man out of prison only six years after he was arrested. She was growing in Christ every day! She was thriving! She was living life to its fullest! That's when God ripped her away from us. One second, she was there…the next, she was gone. She died, and there was not a thing I could do about it. I made it a point to find him and bring him to justice. That man ran, but I went after him. I finally found him in Ohio and called the police. He was taken back to Texas and stood trial. He was found guilty. When the prisoners found out about his past, he didn't last but three months. The inmates gave him their own form of judgement Strangely, I still felt robbed of justice. Had the system not released him so early, she would still be alive. God and I had it out for months before I finally walked away."

"God knows, Ben. He knows your heart and how you feel."

"Right now, we're in the same position. I couldn't do anything to save Joey, and right now I can't do anything to save you."

"We're all dying. It's just a matter of when. And, as far as saving Joey or me, that's not your place. That's God's. John 3:16-17 says, *'For God so loved the world, that He gave His only begotten Son, that whosoever believeth in Him should not perish, but have everlasting life. For God sent not His Son into the world to condemn the world; but that the world through Him might be saved.'* He didn't come here to judge you or your actions, but to save you. There's a story that reflects your concern. Let me see if I can remember it," she said, racking her brain to remember the story. "Luke 23:39 through 43, it says, *'One of the criminals who were hanged there was hurling abuse at Him, saying, 'Are You not the Christ? Save Yourself and us!' But the other responded, and rebuking him, said, 'Do you not even fear God, since you are under the same sentence of condemnation? And we indeed are suffering justly, for we are receiving what we deserve for our crimes; but this man has done nothing wrong.' And he was saying, 'Jesus, remember me when You come into Your Kingdom!' And He said to him, 'Truly I say to you, today you will be with Me in Paradise.'* This man was a criminal who was dying because of his crime. He was literally minutes from death, yet he believed and trusted in Jesus, and Jesus made sure he knew he would be with Jesus that very day in Heaven. Romans 10:9 says, *'If you declare with your mouth, 'Jesus is Lord,' and believe in your heart that God raised Him from the dead, you will be saved.'* He wants you to be with Him in Heaven for all eternity. Only you can make that happen. You have to make a choice. If you don't, you'll end up in that lake of fire. You turned your back on Him, but he's still standing there waiting for you."

"What if you're wrong about this? What if –?"

"Ben, I'm not going to argue semantics with you," Hope said. "If I'm wrong, then I've wasted my life being a good person, doing good things, blessing others in Jesus's name. I will have done good in my life. If I'm right, though, and you choose not to listen, then it's you who will suffer for all eternity."

"Fair enough. I –" Ben started coughing again.

Hope strained to listen. She heard him coughing, gagging, and retching. Then she heard silence. She waited a few moments before calling out, "Ben? Ben!"

◁◁◁◁◁

"WELL, this is day one of being confined to the hotel," Shawn said to Mac. Shawn and Mac shared a bed, and Colby had the other in their room.

"It could be worse," Mac pointed out. "The girls are in the adjoining room, and we're all safe here. No one knows where we are right now."

"And it'll stay that way," Colby said from his bed. "Us staying hidden secures not only our safety, but also allows the others to focus on what they need to without worrying about us."

Shawn nodded. "This is true."

"Think of it as an extended vacation." Colby lay on his side, leaning on one arm. "We can chill out and watch TV all day with the company of three nice ladies."

"That depends," Shawn said.

"What depends?" Mac asked.

"As far as chilling out," Shawn said. "Lindsey's in that group next door."

"Just because you don't get along with her doesn't mean the rest of us don't," Colby pointed out. "If you would just get off your high-horse – both of you – then you may find out just how much you two actually like each other."

"You're delusional!" Shawn snapped.

"Really?" Colby raised an eyebrow. With a slight chuckle, he added, "Me thinks thou doth protest too much."

Shawn chucked a pillow at Colby. "Shut up!"

Catching the pillow, Colby said, "Don't start. We aren't supposed to make too much noise. We need to be good, so the others can do what they need to in order to get everyone out."

"Fine." Shawn huffed, crossing his arms. "We can't be online. We can't rent a video. We can't order out. We can't –"

"We *can* stop complaining," Mac said in a sigh. When Shawn gave him a cross look, Mac said, "We're alive. We know the others are okay as of now. We know our families are safe. I would think talking and watching TV for a few days would be a small sacrifice to help those who need it."

Shawn shrugged. "True. I guess I can tolerate Lindsey for a few days."

"Maybe longer," Colby said, sitting up in his bed, leaning back against the wall. "We'll probably have to follow them until they're done so they can keep an eye on us. Also, so The Professor doesn't find us and use us against them."

"We can help keep an eye on the others as they rescue them," Mac added. "They're not going to go into the different facilities with all of them. Are they?"

"There are a lot of them. I guess it'll depend on their plan," Colby said. "We won't know until they come to pick us up."

Shawn sighed, looking up at the ceiling. "We have to stay here, but be ready when they come."

❧❧❧

THAT MORNING, Wyatt and his crew left the hotel in Maine. "So, we have a plan?" Wyatt asked while he drove the van.

Deanna nodded. "We do."

"Okay, we're not far. Let's get set up," Wyatt said, pulling over in a deserted rest area.

Once they stopped, Deanna and Adam zip-tied Holly and Blake's hands in front of them. Wyatt taught them in the hotel how to break free from them when it was time. After Deanna and Adam zip-tied Holly and Blake, they blindfolded them.

When they got settled, Wyatt resumed driving. The seat behind Wyatt consisted of Deanna with Blake, and then Adam and Holly behind them. Wyatt had a baseball cap and sunglasses on to disguise himself from the camera. He was grateful for the bright sunlight that morning, making both the cap and glasses seem necessary.

Pulling up to the gate, the security guards stopped them. "Please state your business," he said.

"Hey, Carl," Deanna said from the second seat. "These are the two Professor Roth sent us to bring back. We're using that guy as a driver. We'll take care of him later."

"Understood." Carl nodded. "Go on through."

Carl raised the heavy wooden gate, and the van continued down the road toward the facility. There was a second set of gates made of metal, but during business hours, the wooden gate was the only one used.

"How long do we need to keep these things on?" Holly asked. "It's extremely difficult to focus with the blindfold on."

"Trust me. I'll be with you," Adam promised, giving her hand a gentle squeeze. "Listen for my cue to break your ties. I'll pull your blindfold. Deanna will do the same for Blake."

"This is a huge test of trust. Don't burn us on this," Blake warned.

Deanna clicked her tongue. "I thought we were beyond this."

"We are. Just making our position clear," Blake said. "Imagine if you were us in this scenario."

"Fair enough," Adam agreed.

"We're pulling in," Wyatt said, pulling into a parking spot. "I'll stay in the van while you two take in the other two. That way, I can keep the van running. I have my gun loaded, along with extra magazines in here with me. You just get everyone clear of the building, and I'll handle the rest."

"Agreed," Deanna said. Turning toward Adam, she asked, "Ready?"

"Let's go," he said and scooted on the seat toward the door.

Adam helped Holly, while Deanna helped Blake. They guided them toward the building.

As they walked across the parking lot, Wyatt prayed for strength for the four and that everyone would get rescued without bloodshed.

⟐⟐⟐⟐

"WE'RE HEADING INTO THE BUILDING," Deanna said in a low voice to the other three. "Holly, Adam will guide you. You two go get the others, so we have more offense gifts. Adam can link to Blake, and we'll let you know where we are. Blake, you're with me. I need you to stay in communication with Adam. That way, no one will feel left out."

"I feel good about this plan," Holly said.

"Me too," Blake agreed. "Adam, stay in communication."

"Got it," Adam said. "We're all in this together."

Holly nodded. "Until the very end."

⟐⟐⟐⟐

AFTER ADAM AND HOLLY LEFT, Deanna and Blake stood in the hall for a moment so Blake could find Ben and Hope. "They're here," Blake said. "I can sense Mom. She looks like she's in one of the rooms I saw you in when you were little. It's got a lot more rust and looks super worn out."

"The isolation rooms. I know where they are," Deanna said confidently. "If there's no one in the stairwell, I'll loosen you blindfold so you can see. Until then, everyone will think you're my captive if I keep you bound."

"Agreed," he said, so they headed toward the stairwell.

Making their way to the stairwell door, Deanna was careful not to run Blake into anything. "Stairs," she said as they started down the stairs. When they hit the first landing, she asked, "Is there anyone else in this stairwell?"

"No," Blake said after a moment.

Deanna adjusted his blindfold so it still covered his eyes but allowed him to see out the bottom so he would not trip on the stairs. "Is that good?" she asked.

"That'll work."

Heading down three flights of stairs, they finally reached the basement. Deanna fought the flashbacks as she stared at the metal door leading to what was her most horrific nightmare growing up. She gulped as her heart raced.

"May I?" Blake asked.

"Please," she said, feeling like she wanted to throw up.

Blake pushed a feeling of courage toward her until he felt her confidence. "Ready?" he asked.

"Thank you," she acknowledged. "Question is, are you ready?"

"Yes."

Deanna concentrated on the lock mechanism of the door until she heard the all too familiar *Ch'clink* of the lock release.

They walked into silence. Too silent.

"Go ahead and release your zip ties," Deanna said, removing his blindfold.

He released himself and looked around, fighting back the acid of vomit wanting to come up from the stench of the floor of rooms. It smelled of a myriad of bodily fluids mixed with bleach.

"What do they do to people down here?" he asked, shaking his head in dismay. "This whole place feels very heavy."

"You don't want to know," Deanna said. "I need you to tell me which rooms they're in?"

"Mom's in room four."

Deanna gulped. "Did you say she was in four?"

"Yes. I can't see anything in Dad's mind."

"I was often held in four," she said quietly.

"I'll keep you focused if you want?" Blake offered.

"Please…and thank you," Deanna said as they neared room number four. "There are ten rooms," she continued. "Each of us was assigned the room by our birth order. Hope is in my old room."

Blake rested his hand on Deanna's shoulder and gave it a gentle squeeze. "We get everyone rescued, and you won't have to ever see it again."

"Here's hoping," she said on a sigh. "Stay alert to anyone coming our way. Can you do double-duty?"

"I got it," Blake said. "You just get them released."

Ch'clink The door opened for Hope's room.

"Mom!" Blake said, horrified, running into the room. He pulled his knife out of his pocket and released the zip ties on Hope. "Can you stand?" She was pale and shaking.

"Are you real?" she asked, resting her hands on either side of his face. "Blake? Son? Are you really here?"

"Yes."

"Ben's a couple doors down," she said, staring into his eyes.

"Got it," Deanna said, and left the room. "That's Freya's old room."

"Holly's here too," Blake explained, helping her up. "Adam and Deanna are helping us."

When he walked out of the room, he saw Deanna working on Ben's door. *Ch'clink.*

The door released. When Deanna pushed it open, she gasped.

The smell. The flashbacks. How Hope looked was bad enough, but what Ben looked like…she ran to the sink and threw up.

"Mom, stay here," Blake said, hearing Deanna vomiting in the sink. He rested Hope against the door.

Blake stood in the doorway of Ben's room, momentarily stunned. There was blood all over Ben's clothing and the floor around his chair. It was dripping from his nose, mouth, and ears. He was pale, and his eyes were sunken with black circles around them.

"What did they do to you?" Blake asked, choking back the tears. He knelt down, releasing Ben from the zip-ties securing him to the chair.

Deanna wiped her mouth as she looked over at Blake and Ben. "Is he alive?"

"No," Blake said, doing his best to control not only his emotions, but also Deanna and Hope's.

"He reaffirmed his relationship with Christ about thirty minutes ago," Hope said, holding onto the doorway to stay upright.

"We were so close," Blake said, discouraged.

"Ben fought the poison for as long as possible. He fought the Lord too. At the last minute, he decided he wanted to be with us when he died, so he made things right with Christ."

"Good," Blake said. "At least something good came out of it." Standing, he then turned to Hope. "We need to get you out of here."

"What about Holly?" Hope asked.

"She and Adam have their own job. They're going after the others. Our job was to get the pair of you out. Dad's just a shell. If you help me get her to the van, I'll come back in and help you with the others?" Blake offered Deanna.

"Our job was to get Hope and Ben. Let Adam and Holly do their job," Deanna countered. "Come on. Let's get Hope safe. There's nothing we can do for him."

Blake wrapped one of Hope's arms around his shoulder and had her lean on him.

"No." Deanna stopped him. "Figure out a way to carry her. She'll move too slowly this way. We'll get caught."

Blake glanced at Hope for a solution.

"Carry me fireman style," Hope suggested. "I know you're strong enough. When we get to the parking lot, as Deanna said, Wyatt will cover us."

"Okay," Blake agreed. He picked up Hope, flipping her over his shoulder. He struggled to keep Deanna focused while carrying Hope and paying attention to anyone coming their way.

"Hopefully, Adam and Holly are doing what they're supposed to be doing and will provide a distraction enough for us to get out with her," Deanna said, holding the door to the stairwell open. "It's a long way up."

"I know. Let's go," Blake groaned, carrying Hope up three flights of stairs. With all the weight she lost over the last few weeks, she was lighter than he expected, but still weighed quite a bit.

TIME BOMB

"Everything has its beauty, but not everyone sees it."
Confucius

The girls woke up in the hotel. "What time is it?" Lindsey asked as she had a bed to herself.

Stretching and yawning, Tanya, who shared a bed with Megan, looked at her watch and said, "It's nine. We have thirty minutes before breakfast is closed."

"What if I go get breakfast this morning?" Lindsey asked, getting out of bed. "We can alternate who goes to get it each day. That way, we're not down there in a cluster, and it's a different person each time."

"That's a great idea," Megan mumbled as she rolled back toward the wall and covered her head with the pillow. "Thanks."

"That'll work," Tanya agreed. "I'll get tomorrow."

"I have a pretty good idea of what y'all like," Lindsey said, grabbing her clothes to change in the bathroom. When she finished, she headed down to the breakfast area, only to see

Shawn already down there loading a tray for the boys. Picking up a tray, she mentioned, "Fancy meeting you down here."

"Glad to know y'all are up," he said, taking the waffle from the maker and refilling it for another one. "The eggs are questionable," he said quietly, so the hotel staff member watching them from the doorway of the kitchen did not hear him.

"Is that the only thing I should avoid?" she asked.

"The rest should be safe. Well, the sausage is questionable too."

Noticing he had bacon on the plates and no sausage, she decided to follow suit. Starting the toast, she grabbed three yogurts, three bananas, and three cups of orange juice.

"Your crew doesn't drink coffee?" Shawn asked, grabbing the waffle from the maker and replacing it with batter for the last one.

"No. Trying to avoid that. I do need to grab a soda for Meg. Can you watch this for me?"

"Sure. Machine is down the hall."

"No need," the lady watching the teens said. "What kind?"

"Dr Pepper?" Lindsey asked.

The lady left and returned with three cans of Dr Pepper. "Will this work?"

"Yes! Thank you!" Lindsey said, grateful.

"See ya upstairs," Shawn said to Lindsey after pulling the last waffle from the maker. Turning toward the lady watching them, he added, "Thank you very much."

The lady grinned. "My pleasure!"

Lindsey went to work making a waffle each for the girls while she loaded the toast, butter, syrup, and bacon onto the plates on the tray. After she finished, she headed upstairs.

Kicking the door with her foot to knock, she was relieved when Tanya quickly opened the door. "Thank you," Lindsey said, grateful. "If everyone's dressed, the boys are up," she said, setting the tray on the dresser.

Megan shuffled out of the bathroom with her shorts and t-shirt on. As she walked by Lindsey, Lindsey slid a can of Dr Pepper into her hands. Megan mumbled a word of thanks and headed back to bed. Setting the can on the nightstand, she huddled under the covers and covered her head, falling back to sleep.

Lindsey and Tanya snickered as Tanya quietly knocked on the adjoining door to the boy's room. Greeted by a smiling Colby, Tanya remarked, "You're a morning person."

"We've been awake for a while," he explained. Getting a good look at Megan, he quietly offered, "Y'all can come over here so she can stay asleep."

"We'll take you up on that," Tanya said, grabbing her breakfast. Lindsey followed suit as she fell in step behind Tanya.

"You can use my bed," Colby offered. "I'll sit at the desk."

"Thank you," Tanya said, sitting down. "How'd y'all sleep?"

"Slept like a rock, but been praying since six-thirty for the others," Colby said, resting his crossed ankles on the bed, using his lap to rest his plate.

"What stinks is we won't know anything until they get back here," Mac said.

"If they get back here," Lindsey added. "We really won't know anything at all. We just have to sit here, pray, and wait."

"That's a great attitude," Shawn grumbled.

"You were nice downstairs," Lindsey said. "Did someone pee in your orange juice?"

"No. I just hate not knowing anything."

"We're along for the ride on this one. It's out of our control," Tanya said, taking a bite of her waffle.

"All of it's out of our control," Lindsey added.

"None of it has been in our control," Mac countered. "Ever. That's God's department."

"I, for one, am glad it's not in my hands," Lindsey said.

"There are so many emotions and lives mixed up in this. I'm grateful God has this covered!"

"Agreed!" Tanya said.

Megan shuffled into the room, looking rough. She made her way to the bed. Tanya and Lindsey made room for her, so she lay down next to them. "I heard y'all talking," she mumbled, laying on Colby's pillow.

Mac smirked at her state. "Not a morning person?"

"No. And I left my Dr Pepper in the other room," she said in a groan.

"I got it," Mac said, getting off the bed.

Heading into the girl's room, he easily found the Dr Pepper. It was right next to Megan's Bible. A twinge of guilt ripped through him. She not only thought to bring it but also obviously did her devotions. It had been ages since he did devotions. The more he got to know Megan, the more he admired her.

Grabbing the Dr Pepper, he returned to the room.

⟨▪⟩⟨▪⟩⟨▪⟩⟨▪⟩

ADAM AND HOLLY made their way down the hall, leaving Blake and Deanna.

"What am I walking into?" Holly asked quietly.

"It's a room we all share," Adam explained, guiding her by holding her arm. "There'll be single beds on each side of the room. The girls sleep on one side, and the boys on the other. It's always been that way. Since this is our space, they may not like me walking in without Deanna. Let me do the talking."

"I have no problem with that," Holly agreed.

"Where are you taking her?" a security guard asked, stopping Adam and Holly.

"Honestly?" Adam cocked his head to the side. "Where do you think I'm taking her?" When the guard did not respond, Adam sighed, shaking his head. "This is one of those taken at birth. I'm taking her to The Professor. Unless you want to be the one to explain why I'm late, I strongly suggest you let me take her."

Putting his hands up in surrender, he continued down the hall in the opposite direction Holly and Adam headed.

"How many people are around us?" Holly asked.

"There are a lot."

"How are we going to get everyone out?"

"We have to provide a distraction anyway, so we'll get out amongst the chaos. Remember, Freya and Gemma together are as strong as Deanna. Bells is like me."

"Bells?" Holly asked.

"That's our nickname for Isabelle."

"Cute," Holly said. "I like it."

"We're the only ones allowed to call her that for now. Give the others time to get to know you two. Then they'll relax around you. Now, Eddie'll be the tricky one to get out," Adam explained. "He's in a wheelchair."

"I can lift him. Remember, I'm actually stronger than Deanna. Between the three of us, we'll get everyone out," Holly said confidently.

"I'll make sure Bells projects courage and confidence," Adam explained. "As a matter of fact, I'm going to be quiet for a few. I'm going to talk to her."

"Go for it. The more of a head's up they have, the less we'll have to explain when we get there."

"Agreed," Adam said.

While they walked in silence, Holly prayed they would remain invisible to those who could do them harm and that everyone would get out safely.

As they walked into the stairwell, Adam stopped Holly. "Here," he said, taking her blindfold off. "Keep your hands bound in case we run into someone."

"Thank you."

Resting his hands on her shoulders, he said, "Thank you for what you're doing and are going to do."

"They're our family too."

"Blake and Deanna are on their way out."

Holly's face lit up. "They found Mom and Dad?"

"They did. Hope is really sick."

"And, Dad?"

Adam shook his head. "I'm sorry."

Holly gasped. She closed her eyes, taking a deep breath. With tears brimming her eyes, hate and anger took over before sadness had a chance to rest. Looking at Adam, she promised, "We will get everyone else out. I swear to you."

"I don't doubt it. I told you about Ben so you know I won't hold anything back, and we can trust each other."

"Thank you."

"Ready? They're up two floors."

Holly nodded. While she had a determined look in her eyes, she struggled between anger, hurt, and determination. She knew what she needed to do. "Hold my hands. Only two floors?" Holly confirmed.

"Yes," Adam said, taking her hands into his.

"Is there anyone in the staircase or near one?"

"Near one, but no one in. Why?"

"Hold on," Holly said. Looking toward the desired level, she levitated her and Adam up the two flights. When he raised an eyebrow, she explained, "No use wasting time or energy climbing two flights of stairs. Besides, we need to get out of here before Professor Roth knows we're here."

"I agree," he said, and they headed through the door of the dorm floor. Closing his eyes, Adam listened intently. Hearing no one but the other teens, he released Holly from her zip ties.

She followed him as they headed partway down the hall to the door on the left side of the hallway. When they walked into the room, Gemma and Freya threw their arms around Adam.

Freya and Gemma, Holly guessed, were about five-foot-eight or nine. Their frame was slim, and their long, wavy, light-brown hair hung to their mid-back. Freya had her hair in a high ponytail, while Gemma had her hair down, parted to the side. Their fair skin set off their grayish-blue eyes.

"Where's Deanna?" Isabelle asked. Holly thought Isabelle was really pretty with her straight, dark-brown hair, which was all one length and hung about four to five inches below her shoulders. Her dark-brown eyes were set off by her fair skin as well. She looked to be about the same height as Lindsey.

"She's with Blake and Hope," Adam explained. "We have to get the rest of you out. Then, we're heading to get the others." Looking at Eddie, he said to Freya and Gemma, "Can you guys give him a lift down the stairwell? They won't expect us to take him out that way."

"Do they know you're here?" Gemma asked.

"Oh yes," Isabelle said, rolling her eyes. "When Adam sent thoughts to me, I searched for the security guard. He alerted the others Adam was here with Holly. He didn't mention Deanna or Blake."

"How are we getting out of here?" Eddie asked. Eddie looked to be around Blake's height but had more weight on him. His blue eyes were what stood out to Holly, with his fair skin and dark-brown hair. Holly was amazed. When put together, the group actually did look like siblings, despite being from different mothers. There were various featured that matched other features.

"There's a fifteen-passenger van outside waiting for us," Adam said. Then his eyes widened as he gasped.

"What's wrong?" Holly asked, as they walked out into the hallway.

"The Professor and several guards are in the stairwell," Isabelle explained.

"The Professor is not happy," Adam added. "He's swearing

at the guard for letting me pass without bringing Holly to him. Be prepared, folks. We have company," he finished, just as the door to the floor flew open.

Holly looked up to see a handsome, distinguished-looking, older gentleman. He had stark brown eyes and longer black hair that hung to about his shoulder, with a thin frame. While his featured were handsome, his eyes were sinister. She could sense the darkness in his soul without him saying a word. Narrowing her eyes at him, she breathed out his name, "Professor Roth."

"Yes! My dear child! When I heard you were here, I knew I had to come to see you at once." He had a smile on his face that Holly could not wait to wipe away. "Where is your brother, Blake?"

Holly crossed her arms. "He's busy."

"Oh, I'm sure Deanna will bring him to me in a few minutes if she's not already in my office." Clapping his hands in delight, he said, "I cannot wait to see what you and your brother can do."

"You'll find out sooner than you realize," Holly said and swiped her hand through the air, sending The Professor, along with at least half the guards, against the wall.

Freya and Gemma stepped forward and swiped the opposite direction, sending the remaining guards into the other wall.

A couple got on their radios calling for backup while the teens made a beeline for the door of the stairwell. Suddenly a gunshot rang through the air, and everyone froze.

"I don't know where you think you're going," The Professor said, getting off the floor, "but you're in my facility!"

Eddie parted the other four teens and wheeled forward. Narrowing his eyes as he raised one arm in the air, he shouted, "Enough!"

The Professor suddenly went into the air. As he hung in the air holding onto his throat, Holly, Gemma, and Freya all looked at each other and shook their heads that it was not them.

"I suggest you have your guards holster their weapons,"

Eddie warned. When The Professor nodded, the guard who fired put his gun back in the holster. Eddie did not take his eyes off The Professor as he shouted, "You have tortured all of us over the years!" When the guards went to get up, he lifted his other arm in the air, and all the guards were plastered against the wall they stood next to, about a foot off the ground, unable to move. "You killed Charlie! I watched over the years as you viciously went after each of us you called your children, pushing everyone beyond their limits. And when we did not comply, you tortured us or our closest sibling. I've seen enough! With a father like you, you can only imagine the hate and anger we have toward you!"

"How are we going to get out of here if there are more coming?" Freya asked.

"Go!" Eddie insisted. "I've got this group."

"No!" Holly said adamantly. "We all go. They killed my dad. The rest of us are all leaving here together. No one gets left behind."

"We got the guards," Freya said as she and Gemma stepped forward. When Eddie released the guards, Freya and Gemma each took half. They brought them about a foot from the wall and then slammed them into the wall, knocking them all out.

"Let's go," Eddie said, keeping a handle on The Professor. The Professor dragged along the ground behind Eddie, grasping his neck as he gasped for air. "This is how we're getting out. I've done the calculations."

"What do you mean you've done the calculations?" Adam asked.

"I have multiple gifts, but I have never shared them with anyone," Eddie explained. Heading into the stairwell, Freya and Gemma lifted Eddie's wheelchair as Eddie kept ahold of The Professor, leaving Holly for any other guards that came their way. "I've worked out every scenario. I saw what he did to all of you over the years. If he truly knew what I could do, he would have never let me leave his side. I've been waiting for just the right time to let him know."

"What all *can* you do?" Isabelle asked, as they levitated the two floors.

"Tell us," Adam said. "I need to know to all the elements, so I know how to help us get out of here."

"I can almost see the future. It's what you do, Adam. We run calculations so fast, we can almost predict the future. I can also do all the things with your mind that you all do."

"From what I've seen, you are the strongest one here," Holly said. "I couldn't do what you did the way you did it."

Reaching the bottom, they were met by ten security officers.

"Let me through," Eddie ordered. Seeming to drag The Professor behind him with one hand without touching him, while operating his wheelchair with the other, Eddie made his way out into the hallway. The Professor's face was an interesting shade of reddish-purple by that point. "If you don't want to see your precious Professor's neck snapped, you will let us all through. The first time I even remotely see a gun drawn, I will take you all down!" Eddie growled.

When the security guards looked toward The Professor, he nodded. They all stepped back, hands in the air.

Heading toward the back door toward the awaiting van, Eddie kept The Professor barely off the ground. His feet kicked out behind him, struggling to get some sort of grip.

"I don't know how you hid it for so long, but I'll take it!" Adam said, relieved they did not have to fight.

"I've almost exploded multiple times," Eddie confessed, "but I needed to wait until the appropriate time that would create the least number of casualties."

"Like a time bomb?" Holly asked.

"Exactly," he agreed.

When they finally reached the door, the security officers were still behind them. Wyatt drove the van over to the door.

Deanna, Blake, and Hope were already in the vehicle. When the van door opened, The Professor struggled even harder at seeing those already in the van.

"Load up," Eddie said. "Just leave me room."

Everyone got in, leaving a seat in the second row where he could put the chair in and still have a spot on the bench seat.

Eddie wheeled over to the door. Keeping his hand behind him, continuing to apply pressure to The Professor's neck, he slowly lifted himself, chair and all, into the van. As it went into the air, three guards lifted their weapons. One fired, hitting Eddie in the arm that was holding The Professor. As soon as he felt the searing bite, Eddie let go with a shout. His chair almost hit the ground before Holly stopped it. Deanna brought it into the van, while The Professor crawled toward his guards, gasping for air.

"Stop them!" The Professor growled though gritted teeth.

Wyatt fired toward the guards through the open sliding door, hitting two each in the shoulders. While Wyatt dropped his gun into his lap to drive, Deanna slammed Eddie's chair into the van. Holly lifted Eddie into the seat while Adam manually collapsed Eddie's chair, and Freya used her gift to secure the door. As soon as the door was closed, Wyatt shoved his foot down on the gas pedal, spinning the tires.

Leaving, they heard the bullets hitting the vehicle. The teens all ducked the gunfire. A few screamed when one of the side windows shattered. As they neared the gate, Wyatt saw the tall metal gates starting to close, so he pushed down on the gas to the floor, splintering the wood barrier blocking the entrance as they went through. The security guard attempted to stop them, firing into the front windshield. He ducked out of the way just in time, so Wyatt barely missed hitting him.

The group was just past the entrance when the tall gates slammed shut. The guard at the gate fired off a few more rounds at the van, barely missing the tires.

"We're clear," Wyatt announced. "They locked themselves in with the gate. Who all is hurt?"

"I am," Eddie said, holding pressure on his bleeding left arm. The others responded in a scattered chorus they were fine.

"Son, I don't know who you are, but that was incredible," Wyatt said to Eddie. "Thanks to you, no one was killed."

"Except Dad," Holly said, reaching forward for Hope's hand. Holly sat beside Eddie in the second seat, with Deanna on her other side. Hope was in the passenger's seat.

Hope grabbed Holly's hand to comfort her. Hope's skin felt cool and clammy to Holly's touch. Hope's normally pleasantly plump features looked sunken at best. Her pupils were dilated, and she continuously kept her eyes shaded with her right arm. While they waited in the van for the others, she kept asking where they were and how they got there. She also continued to ask about Ben.

As they drove down the road, Holly gave her mom's hand a squeeze before she turned her attention to Eddie. "How can I help?" she asked.

"I need the bullet out," Eddie explained. "It's still in there. I could do it, but…" his voice trailed.

"You're not going to like it," Holly warned.

"I don't have a choice. Why couldn't they shoot my legs?" He groaned. "I wouldn't be able to feel those."

"I wish I could give you something for the pain," Wyatt said. "Unfortunately, we have to get out of this area before they track us down. I know Hope needs a hospital too, but we can't stop yet."

Eddie closed his eyes as he lay his head back on the seat. "Just do it."

"I can help," Isabelle offered.

"How?" Holly asked.

"I can take him into his mind," she explained.

"Bells, what will you do if he goes unconscious with you in there?" Adam asked.

"Come in with me," she said with a shrug. "You can pull me out."

"No," Eddie said. "You'll both get stuck."

"I can push a calm feeling onto you?" Blake offered.

"What if we just knock him out?" Deanna asked.

"How, pray tell, do you expect to do that?" Wyatt asked.

"Don't ask a question you don't want to know the answer to," she said flatly.

"What if you just do it already?" Eddie growled, still clasping his bloody arm.

Holly did not respond verbally. She held his arm with one hand while she braced her hand over the top of the area. After a few agonizing moments of yells and screams from Eddie, he gratefully passed out, and she was able to get the bullet out. "How do I stop the bleeding?" Holly asked after the bullet was out and resting in her hand.

"Here," Blake said, handing her a white t-shirt from his bag under the seat.

"Can I tear it?" Holly asked.

"Yeah. I don't want it back."

Holly tore the sleeves off the shirt and used those to cover the wound, before she tightly tied what was left of the shirt around Eddie's arm. "There," she said, satisfied.

"Holly? Is that you?" Hope asked.

"Hope, please just hold my hand and get some rest," Wyatt said. Then he loudly added, "Why don't y'all get some rest? We're fixin' to have a long drive ahead of us."

MOMENTS IN TIME

It is not the length of life, but depth of life.” Ralph Waldo Emerson

“The nerve of them coming in here and taking my children!” The Professor shouted as he paced his office.

Alex sat on the couch, watching him pace. Knowing he needed to blow off steam, she let him rant for over ten minutes.

He finally stopped and stared at her. “Eddie has gifts! That boy has sat for sixteen years…sixteen years! He’s had gifts this entire time! How did I not know about them? How did he hide them from me this entire time?”

“I honestly have no idea. No one saw any telekinetic activity from him when he was too little to hide it?”

“No. They were more concerned with Isabelle, Freya, Gemma, Deanna, and Chris to probably notice Eddie. He used that to his advantage at an infantile stage of life.” Going over to her, he knelt in front of her to make his point, “Do you know what kind of power it takes for a baby to process that? His mind must be fascinating!"

"I honestly have no idea. What all can he do?"

"He's like Adam and the others combined. He had me by the throat, as he had the security officers plastered against the wall. That takes an immense amount of power."

"You almost sound as if you admire him," Alex observed.

"I want him back!" he growled. He got up and resumed pacing. "If he is that strong, the others must be that strong as well." Spinning toward her, he added, "We must push the others to see just how strong they truly are!"

"Daddy, you've pushed those children to the point of exhaustion."

"Obviously not! Who else is holding out on me?"

Alex stood.

"Where are you going?"

"Well, knowing you, you're going to want some time to formulate a plan. I'm going to go pack. I have a feeling I won't be here for long since the kids are no longer here."

He winked at her. "Knew I raised a smart one!"

⧫⧫⧫⧫

AFTER WATCHING their fourth movie for the day, with the girls on one bed, Mac and Shawn on the other, and Colby on the couch, Shawn shut the television off. "I understand why we have to be here. I just wish there was some way they could let us know they're okay."

"There's not," Megan said. "Any electronic communication from this point forward will be tagged. While we could sneak a few in on a random account before, now that Professor Roth knows everyone is working together, he'll have everything tagged and flagged. He'll be looking for some type of communication."

Shawn groaned. "This sucks! Sincerely!"

"At least we're safe," Lindsey pointed out. "Our families are, too. That's the whole point of this. It won't be forever. Just relax until they come to get us."

"What happens after they get the others away? What are they going to do with us?" Tanya asked.

"Pretty sure they'll take us with them," Megan said. "I don't think they'll want to come back here to get us."

"Too bad we don't have any games," Mac said, shifting to a more comfortable position. "I would even play *Go Fish* right now."

Tanya propped her chin on her hand. "We're not supposed to go anywhere, so a store is out."

"I do have a deck of cards," Megan offered. "I only have one deck, though. I would have picked up more when we got the hair color, but I wasn't expecting to be sequestered to the hotel. Maybe when we go, we can stop at a gas station. I'll pick up a couple more decks, along with some candy of some kind to play *Texas Hold 'Em.*"

"Now that sounds like a plan!" Shawn said, satisfied. Turning the television back on, he began scrolling through the movies once again. "Next movie?"

⫘⫘⫘

THE GROUP in the van were driving for about an hour before anyone said anything. All were on edge.

"How are you feeling, Hope?" Wyatt asked, gently squeezing her hand, while he used his other to drive.

"Huh? What? Where's Ben? He's not doing well," Hope mumbled.

"Mom, Dad's gone," Holly said quietly. "Don't you remember?"

"Holly?"

"Yes."

"What are you doing here? Professor Roth is a bad man!" Hope said, wide-eyed. "He'll do terrible things to you if he finds you!"

"Mom, you're safe. You're not there anymore. Please come back to us?" Holly encouraged.

"I could take those memories away if you want?" Isabelle offered.

Blake shook his head. "No. If you take that away, you'll take away the memory of Ben coming back to Christ, but thank you."

"What do you mean?" Isabelle asked.

Holly turned toward the seat behind her, which held Blake, Isabelle, and Adam. Freya and Gemma were in the last row with the bags. "Do you know who Jesus Christ is?"

"Remember who you're talking to," Deanna gently reminded Holly.

"Right." Holly nodded. "That may take a little longer than we have right now. I'll talk to you more about it later. Just know it's a matter of life and death that she remembers. I agree with Blake. She needs to keep the memories."

Isabelle shrugged. "Okay. If you change your mind, let me know."

"We will. Thank you."

Feeling the tension within the group, Blake sent out a feeling of peace. Then he cleared his throat before he suggested, "Since we don't know everyone, I think introductions are in order. What if we say our name and our gift? That way, we are all aware of what we have together."

"Together?" Freya asked. "Are you coming with us to get the others?"

"No," Blake said. With a smile and a wink, he corrected her, "You're coming with *us* to get the others. We're all in this together. We may not have been raised together, but we are all a family."

"How can you say that?" Gemma asked, putting her hair in a ponytail.

"Our father is the same." Blake shrugged. "We're all related by blood."

"Let me take a crack at this," Adam suggested. When Blake nodded, Adam explained, "Out in the real world, things are run differently. We're learning just how differently. We all know we're going to have some adjusting to do, but just like those in the other facilities are our brothers and sisters, so are Blake and Holly."

Freya nodded. "I can see that. It makes sense."

"That's a good way of looking at it," Holly said.

"So, what if we tell each other our gifts and names?" Blake asked again.

"I'll start," Freya said, a twinkle in her eyes. "I'm Freya, and this is my twin, Gemma."

"We both have the gift of telekinesis," Gemma added. "We also have a mental connection with each other only."

"Good to know," Blake said. "I'm Blake. My gifts consist of projecting feelings and now reading minds. Also, Adam showed me how to remove thoughts as well. Oh! I can also project my thoughts onto Holly, and she can with me."

"Really?" Freya asked, raising her eyebrows in surprise. "I thought that was a twin thing?"

"We were raised as twins," Holly said. "I guess because we've been inseparable, the bond grew over the years."

"They literally have their own language," Wyatt said from the driver's seat. "Blake and Holly don't even have to talk to know what the other is thinking. By the way, I'm Wyatt. No gifts. Just the County Sherriff down in Willow Bend, Texas area. I actually live in Willow Bend."

Freya and Gemma looked at him, wide-eyed.

Seeing the terror in their eyes, Wyatt elaborated, "Hope is my fiancé. I helped raise Blake and Holly. My intention is to rescue y'all from that cretin and get you settled into homes around the county. Close enough, yet a little space to grow into your own."

"Oh. Okay," Freya said, breathing a sigh of relief.

"Don't worry. I know all about Professor Roth and that place. I give you my word I'll use everything within me to get all y'all out," Wyatt vowed.

"I don't doubt that," Isabelle said. "I can sense you are a truthful and honorable man. Thank you."

"Anytime, young lady," Wyatt said with a smile.

"Blake, you forgot about how you can push thoughts onto others," Holly said.

"Oh yeah!" he said, remembering. "That too."

"Wait! What does that mean?" Isabelle asked.

"I can make someone do what I want by pushing the thought onto them. They have the free will to not do it, but only Wyatt, Mom, Dad, and Holly have figured out how to combat it," Blake said.

"So, almost like persuasion, but not vocally?" Adam asked.

"Yes."

"You also projected into our minds while we were unconscious," Deanna said. "The others can't do that."

"Wait!" Isabelle said, holding her hand up. "You went into unconscious minds?"

"I did," Blake confirmed.

"He did more than that. He also pushed memories into our minds while we were unconscious," Adam corrected.

"Wow! I didn't know that was possible!" Isabelle said, amazed.

"Honestly, I didn't know there was a danger," Blake admitted.

"I'm impressed," Isabelle said. "Well, I'm Isabelle. Those close to me call me Bells. If you want to, you can call me that too."

"I would like to," Holly said. "I think it's a cute nickname."

"Thank you," Bells said, her cheeks slightly flushed. "My, um," she nervously cleared her throat, "my gift is that of the mind. I can sense people. I can also project feelings like Blake, and can remove thoughts from others. That's a skill I would be happy to help you sharpen," she offered to Blake.

"That would be great. Playing with people's minds makes me extremely nervous," Blake said.

"Once you know what you're doing, it's easy. However, it's never to be taken lightly. We only remove the memory if it will scar someone for life," Bells explained.

"Kind of like with Holly," Adam added.

"What about me?" Holly asked.

"Don't worry about it," Blake said, easing her mind. "I was there. He did it for your benefit."

"Did what?" Holly asked.

"Seriously, don't make me tell you," Blake said. "I don't want to bring it back up again."

"We all agreed," Wyatt pointed out.

"Okay." She shrugged. "It's just a little nerve-racking to know y'all know something about me that I've apparently forgotten."

"Just trust me?" Blake asked.

"I do."

"Good."

"I'm Holly," she said. "My gift is telekinesis, like Deanna."

"Not like Deanna," Deanna corrected. "You're stronger than I am."

Holly's cheeks flushed in embarrassment.

"Freya and Gemma together are as strong as I am," Deanna continued. "It would take all three of us to match your strength."

"Really?" Holly asked, surprised.

"Yes! Good grief, girl! You have no idea of just how strong you really are," Deanna went on. "If you got really angry, I promise you could match Eddie over there."

"Seriously?" Holly asked, her jaw dropping. "He's really strong!"

"It seems he's stronger than all of us," Adam said, glancing at the sleeping Eddie. "The turkey kept it a secret this entire time. Of course, now that I think about it, some of the things he's said over the years now makes sense. By the way, I'm Adam, and you know my gifts."

"We do," Gemma said.

"Um." Holly nervously tucked her strawberry-blond hair behind her ear. Glancing at her mom to make sure she fell back to sleep, Holly then quietly asked, "What happened to Dad?"

"It's something I'm trying to block for the moment," Blake said, slumping in his seat, crossing his arms.

"He was poisoned," Deanna said, keeping an eye on Blake.

"More than poisoned!" Blake snapped. "He had blood all over his clothes and the floor around him! He looked like he got the tar beaten out of him! He looked like he was melting in the chair. I just –" Blake shook his head. "And before you ask, no, I want to keep that memory. Next time I see that man, I want to make sure he faces justice!"

"Blake," Wyatt warned.

"Not by killing him."

"That's the only way he'll face any kind of justice," Bells piped up. "He's never paid for any of his crimes."

"You don't know the half of it." Adam shook his head. "His crimes are crimes against humanity itself."

"Tell us about Ben," Bells said, projecting a feeling of calmness to everyone in the van.

Holly got a smile on her face at the myriad of memories that flooded her mind. "There's so much to tell. He homeschooled us. He taught us to use and control our gifts, getting stronger as we got older. He never pushed. He guided."

"He had a great sense of humor, too," Wyatt said. "Some of the one-liners he popped off with had us laughing for hours!"

"Yes, a lot of inside jokes came from him," Holly agreed.

"He was the reason we weren't raised by that piece of –"

"Blake!" Wyatt cut Blake off. "Language!"

"Yes, sir," Blake relented. "Sorry."

"It would honestly be a kindness to the world to put that man down," Adam said. "Trust me. I've studied men like him."

"It would dishonor Ben," Blake said finally understanding what Wyatt was trying to tell him. "Killing another for justice won't bring that person back."

"No. It won't," Wyatt said. "It'll also be something I don't even think Bells or Adam could take away. That feeling of taking another human life will always remain. When he goes before God, God will take vengeance. Nothing is unseen by The Lord God Almighty."

"True." Blake sighed. "I just miss him. That man took our dad away."

"Professor Roth is your dad," Freya corrected. "Just like he's our dad."

"No. He's our sperm donor," Blake told Freya. "A dad would never treat his kids the way that man treated you."

"How would you know how he treated us?" Gemma asked.

"I saw it," Blake said.

"In our minds," Adam explained. "This is what I mentioned earlier. We were sedated for almost two weeks in the hospital. During that time, Blake found out what we faced by diving into our minds. He also showed us how he and Holly were raised."

"I see," Gemma said, sitting back in her seat. "May I point out that seeing it and living it are two different things."

"Exactly my point," Blake said. "Seeing it was bad enough. You should never have to call that man *Dad*. He hasn't earned that title. Ben did. He may not have been our birth father, but he was our dad…and always will be remembered as such. He was a kind man. He was an honorable man. He was a man of integrity.

He told us he wished he could have taken all of us. Unfortunately, he and Mom only got away with Holly and me."

"However, now that we're getting y'all away from him, you'll experience what real love and living life to the fullest is like," Wyatt added.

"Starting with chocolate," Holly said, pointing to the gas gauge that was creeping ever so quickly toward empty.

Wyatt laughed as he looked up in time to get off the highway to go to a gas station. When they pulled in, Wyatt said, "Holly and Deanna can go in, but everyone else please stay inside?"

"Eddie's in our way," Holly pointed out.

"We got it," Blake said, gently pushing Adam toward the door.

While Wyatt filled the van with gas, Blake and Adam went inside to get snacks.

"Wow!" Adam said, wide-eyed, as he stood in front of the snack aisle.

"Put your shirt out to hold these," Blake said, grabbing several candy bars, chips, and various other snacks.

"They're going to lose their minds," Adam said in a chuckle, while Blake put the sodas in his shirt to carry.

Blake grinned. "This is just the beginning of a new life for y'all."

"Blake, I'm really sorry about your dad. I wish we could have gotten back sooner."

"You weren't in control of that. Technically, we were. We're the ones who kept y'all knocked out for so long."

"He seemed like a really good guy. I feel like I knew him by the memories you put in my mind."

"There was oh so much more. He was a good man taken too soon."

"According to you, it was just in time," Adam countered.

"What do you mean?" Blake asked.

"Two things: number one – it's not the length of life, but the depth of life; number two – you made it clear not to take the memory of Ben accepting Christ as his Savior away. I was curious, so I looked into this Jesus Christ."

Blake raised an eyebrow. "We were in the van. How did you find out about Christ?"

"Mind reader. Remember?"

Blake raised an eyebrow. "Whose mind did you read?"

"Holly's."

"Without her permission?"

"Habit. I'm used to reading just about everyone's mind around me. It's a bit of a survival instinct. When you were talking about the memory of Ben accepting Christ, you were strong in your conviction. I can't read your mind because you have me blocked, so I looked into Holly's about Jesus Christ. Her sense of Him was stronger than what you vocalized."

"That's something she's passionate about."

"What about you?" Adam asked as they placed all the food on the counter to pay for them.

"Not really wanting to think about it until this is over."

"Is that something you think you should put off? Ben almost waited until it was too late," Adam pointed out.

"That will be thirty-three, thirty," the cashier said.

As Blake handed her thirty-five dollars from his wallet, he said, "What all did you find out about Jesus Christ?"

"I have to admit I was curious. Her conviction was strong," Adam said while the cashier bagged their snacks. "I dove in to see why."

"Got it. Good to know." Blake picked up three bags of various chips and candy, while Adam got the two with the sodas in them. Walking out of the convenience store, Blake said, "What do you think about Jesus Christ and all He's done for you?"

"I think I'm going to be talking to Holly about it once we slow down enough."

"I would talk to Mom or Wyatt about it instead of Holly. We were only at church for one week, before all this chaos hit. Of course, she spent the next few weeks with Colby, so she may know more than I think she does."

"She does," Adam said confidently.

They climbed back into the van. Everyone perked up at their entrance.

"What did you get?" Holly asked.

"I know we should stop and get them to a hospital, but..." Wyatt's voice faded as Eddie groaned in pain.

Eddie's eyes slowly fluttered open. His hand immediately went to his arm. "It hurts," he mumbled on a moan.

"I'm sure. It will," Holly said. She reached over the seat and stuck her hand into one of the bags Blake had on his lap. Pulling out a chocolate bar, she slowly unwrapped it in front of Eddie. "This will make it all better."

"What is that?" he asked, eyeing the candy bar. "It smells amazing!"

Deanna smiled. "Wait until you taste it!"

Holly handed Eddie the open chocolate bar. Freya and Gemma watched in anticipation of his reaction.

"Oh! Oh my!" Eddie groaned in pleasure. "Yes. This makes up for the pain."

"Um, can I...I mean, can we please have one?" Freya asked, looking at Eddie's chocolate bar as she licked her lips.

"Sure," Blake said, handing them each one before passing them out to the others. "Also, this is soda, sometimes called as pop, depending on where you're from." He handed each one a soda before he got one for himself. He also passed some snacks forward for Wyatt and Hope.

"We were talking inside," Blake started. Adam nervously glanced over at Blake to see where he was going with his statement. "Adam mentioned a phrase that's now stuck in my head. He said, *it's not the length of life, but the depth of life.* I feel like y'all have not lived your lives until now. Meanwhile, Dad's depth of life was vast."

"It was," Wyatt agreed.

"He saved us and poured into us," Holly added.

"I know from what we've experienced with you all up to now, just how much life we haven't lived," Adam said.

"I agree. Those memories you shared with us showed me so much," Deanna concurred. "I'm excited to see where we go from here."

"What are those little bags?" Eddie asked, keeping an eagle eye on one of the other bags on the seat between Blake and Adam.

"These," Blake said, pulling out one of the tiny chip bags, "are called potato chips."

"Wait. What are those?" Deanna asked. "We haven't had those yet."

"With chips, they have all sorts of delicious flavors from which to choose," Blake said, passing each teen a different flavor. "I got a little of everything. The best way to find out if you like them is to share and see which one is your favorite."

"You're fixin' to turn them into junk food junkies," Wyatt said on a chuckle.

Blake shrugged. "Just sharing the joy of what they haven't experienced yet. They need to be real teens."

As each teen shared the chips and snacks, the delight on their faces brought absolute bliss to Blake's heart. Getting a glimpse of what their past was like, he wanted to ensure happiness as much as possible for them from this point forward.

DOWN TIME

"Lost time is never found again." Benjamin Franklin

Driving through the night, Wyatt pushed to get back into Philadelphia before he took Hope to the hospital. It killed him to watch her have hallucinations even when she was sleeping. However, he could not risk stopping earlier and The Professor finding them too quickly for her to get the care she needed.

He calculated it out. It took them a good eight hours to get from where he dropped the Willow Bend teens off at the hotel to where they spent the night in Maine. At this point, he still had a good hour before they reached Philadelphia, the hospital, and the safety of the hotel.

ALEX PACKED HER BAGS. Knowing Ben's body was downstairs, but he was not there, her heart was shattered. Despite Ben's warnings to stay away, she still went down to see him after the teens left. She did not expect to see his body still there. She went down to feel close to him again. What she saw in that room will be forever engrained into her mind.

She continued to wipe her tears as she packed. Placing the photo of the two of them in the suitcase, she made sure to tuck it under her clothing in case her father walked into the room. She jumped when she heard an abrupt rap on the door.

"Yes?" she called out.

Her father opened the door. "Are you almost packed?"

"Yes," she said, closing her suitcase. Wiping her face, she turned and faced him. "When do I leave?"

"What is wrong, love? Why the tears?" he asked, actually showing concern. Resting his hands on her shoulders, he continued, "I know you don't like to be separated from me, but that is no reason for tears."

Of course, he would think that! Narcissist! "It's not that," she said dismissively.

"Then what, pray tell, is wrong?"

"I just – I feel upset at everything that happened," she explained. She knew she could not tell him the truth. He would not understand.

Wrapping his arms around her, he said, "I know things seem confusing, but you are stronger than this. We will get those kids back. Don't you worry your pretty little head."

Of course, his concern is for the teens. Looking up at him, she asked, "Daddy? Do you care more about the teens than me?"

Stroking her hair, he shook his head. "No, love. You are the most important thing to me on this planet. You are my pride and joy. Those teens are simply subjects. However, they represent a lot of hard work – years of hard work. I don't want to lose that. That took a lot of precious time from you, and I want it all to be worth it. I want to give you the world. The way to do that is through those children."

Alex took a step back. Straightening her clothes, she looked up at him and asked, "So, if you were not able to keep ahold of them, would you focus on me and those you still have?"

Redness crept from below his collar, slowly filling his face. To her, he looked like a volcano about to erupt. "Why would I stop pursuing my subjects? They are my subjects! They are *mine*! Those who dare to take from me face severe consequences." Pacing her room, he continued, "You are mine. This facility is mine. The Wyoming and Oregon facilities, along with what all is in them are mine." He stopped and stared at her. "No one takes what is mine! No one!"

⟨⟩⟨⟩⟨⟩

"I NEED you all to stay here while I take Hope to the hospital," Wyatt said, pulling up to the hotel. "I'll get y'all rooms up there and sort everyone out, and then I'll take Hope."

"I'll go with you," Holly said. "For safety and to watch Mom while you're in the hotel."

"Good idea. Thank you," Wyatt said, appreciatively.

Wyatt and the others went inside, where he got two more rooms. They were only able to get them on the same floor as the other two rooms. The new rooms were at the other end of the hallway. When the group got upstairs, there was a brief meeting in the Willow Bend girl's room.

"To keep things copacetic, I'm going to move the Willow Bend boy's room, so they adjoin with the Maine boy's rooms. The Maine girls are going to move into here, so they adjoin with the Willow Bend girl's room. Know that I trust y'all. I just think it's the more appropriate way to separate y'all. I'll sleep in the Maine boy's room, while Blake will sleep in the Willow Bend boy's room. Holly will sleep in the Willow Bend girl's room since there are three in there and four Maine girls."

"What about Hope and Ben?" Megan asked.

"Well, um, Hope needs to go to the emergency room. I'm taking her to the hospital. Holly's coming with me. Ben, uh," Wyatt nervously rubbed the back of his neck, "he, uh, didn't make it. We didn't get there in time."

"I see," Megan said, shifting in her seat on Colby's bed. "So, um, are we staying here until Hope is better?"

Wyatt ran his fingers through his hair, letting out a slow breath of air. Then he crossed his arms while leaning on the dresser. "I don't know. I do know have to come back for Hope. I don't want to leave her, but we have to get to those other kids. The Professor's still alive, and he knows what we're doing. He'll be more prepared next time."

"Since he already knows, what if we take a few days to just relax?" Adam asked. "A little downtime. Time where we're not required to perform."

"Time to rest, get to know each other, and regain our strength," Blake added. "One of us also needs to stitch Eddie's arm over there."

"That would be Tanya," Mac said. "She's a skateboarder. She's had plenty of scrapes and cuts over the years."

"Yeah. I got it," Tanya said, getting up to get a needle and thread. "What about alcohol or some type of antiseptic?"

"Here," Wyatt said, getting into the first aid kit he brought. "And, A little downtime'll work. That'll also let me know if Hope's going to be okay."

"Do we get waffles in the morning again?" Deanna asked.

"We've created a monster." Blake rolled his eyes, shaking his head. There were chuckles heard from around the room.

⟐⟐⟐⟐

ALEX BOARDED one plane while The Professor boarded another. Stopping at the top of the stairs, she glanced over her shoulder toward him. He blew her a kiss before entering. She watched as the door closed and the plane taxied.

"Time to go, Alex," Kendrick Holmes said. He was one of the security guards with her. Standing on the steps behind her, he gave her a gentle nudge.

"I know," she said on a sigh. Taking a deep breath, she cleared the remaining steps into the hollow metal tube that was to transport her to Wyoming.

Taking a seat in the front of the plane, she secured her seatbelt.

"Want some company?" Kendrick asked. "You seem down. It's at least a five-hour flight to Cheyenne and then another three-hour drive to Creston. Maybe some company will help clear your head."

"Actually, that would be nice. You guys don't have to sit in the back for this trip."

"Guys!" he yelled to the other three guards. When they looked up, he said, "C'mon up here. Alex needs company."

They happily obliged, taking seats on the other side of the plane, two-by-two while it took off. Once in the air, the group sat around a table at the front of the plane, playing a game of cards.

"What's going on, Alex? You were quiet the entire two-hour drive to Bangor. Now you're on edge. You're normally so calm, cool, and collective," Seth Stevens pointed out. "This edge is not an edge of coolness. It's an edge of distress."

Alex shook her head.

"Alex," Kent Evans said, knowingly, "you know we'll get it out of you before this is over."

Alex sighed, setting two cards down, getting two more from the dealer, Kendrick. No one moved. When she looked up at them, they were staring at her. "Fine," she huffed. "It's just that there's a lot at stake."

"Well, your dad's been working at this for a long time,"

Kendrick said, returning to the game. "We've all got a lot vested in this as well."

"What do you mean?" Alex asked.

"Our lives so far are invested in protecting you and your dad. Those kids also help to protect the pair of you. Without them, we're in trouble."

Alex cocked her head to the side. "What do you mean?"

"If they come after you two, we have no defense," Kendrick explained. "How do you defend against telekinesis or a mind reader?"

"Or worse yet, someone who knows what you're going to do?" Brett Simmons said. "Then there are those who can control your feelings." He shook his head as he replaced one card. "That's just messed up!"

Alex nodded in understanding. "I see your point."

"That's not all you're struggling with," Brett said to Alex. "I've seen you stressed. This is more depressed or down. You almost seem to thrive on stress. When you're stressed, you're like a sharpened tool, ready to slice whomever or wherever needed."

"Surgical," Kendrick acknowledged.

"Exactly! This is something different, though," Brett said. "This is upset."

"How is it you guys know more about me than my own father?" Alex asked. "He thought I was upset about the kids getting away or me being separated from him." When the men burst out in laughter, she asked, "What?"

"Well," Kendrick cleared his throat, "nothing against those kids or your dad, but that's not you. You are an all-business type person. There really isn't much that bothers you. And, honestly, I've only seen you play the dutiful daughter, doing what daddy says all these years. He tells you to go to this place and do this, you do it. He tells you to go there, you do it. Emotionless. This," he gestured toward her, "is anything but emotionless. There is something bothering you at your core."

"I'm struggling," she admitted.

"Why?"

"Ben."

Silence.

"He taught me a lot about family when I was in Texas. I saw what Daddy did to him." She shook her head. Wiping the tear that escaped down her cheek, she mumbled, "He didn't deserve it."

"Did the women deserve what he did to them?" Kendrick asked. When everyone looked at him in shock, he explained, "I don't mean to speak ill of my boss, but honestly, I saw the pictures of those women. I was there for the Oregon women ten years ago. I've watched how he's treated you over the last twelve years I've worked for this company," he said to Alex. "He treats you like an asset, not a daughter. I'm sorry if it offends you. I'm tired of not saying anything. I got tired of hearing him shout at you through the door whenever you called from Texas. I'm tired of seeing the way he treats those kids. Having said all of that, I have a job to do. It's my duty to fulfill that job, and I will do so to the best of my ability…no matter how tired I am of it all. I'm also loyal. I will do everything I can to make sure you're safe."

"Thank you. I appreciate everything you've said. And, don't worry. I won't tell Daddy," she said. "I understand. That's partially what I'm struggling with."

"Alex?" Brett asked. When she looked up at him, he said, "You liked him."

Alex nodded.

"Did you love him?" He asked. Alex looked up at Brett. When their eyes met, he nodded. "I'm sorry. I've seen whatever that stuff he gives them does to people. When you care about them, it makes it that much worse."

"What do you know about it?" Alex asked.

"He liked one of the carriers of the Oregon kids," Kent explained. "We both liked a couple of them. We looked after them while they were pregnant. I still remember what Sienna looked like when I found her in the condo." He shuddered. "I called the clinic. The paramedics cut little Lexi from her dead body. They treated Sienna like an animal, not a human being."

"That's it!" Alex said. "He treats people like an experiment…an animal. Where is his humanity?"

"We'll probably get fired for this conversation," Brett said, "but we hang on for you, not him."

"I appreciate that. I wish there was something I could do to help those under him," she said.

"Treating us like humans help," Kendrick pointed out. When she raised an eyebrow, he said, "You have been cold but never neglected the decency to treat us like human beings. You care."

"Thank you."

"Your father, on the other hand…" Brett's voice trailed off.

"I appreciate your honesty and candid conversation," Alex said. "It's actually refreshing. I thought it was just me. I mean, he's my dad, but I am still struggling on how he handles people and situations."

"One day, there'll be an opportunity for you to stand up and spread your wings," Kendrick said. "Just know we're behind you in whatever steps you take."

⋘⋙

"It's been over an hour since we brought her in," Holly said, glancing at her watch as she and Wyatt sat in the waiting room. "When are they going to tell us something?"

"They will when they know something," Wyatt encouraged.

"I wonder how the others are doing?"

Wyatt shrugged. "Guess we'll find out when we get back."

◁◎▷◁◎▷

AFTER TRADING BEDDING with the Willow Bend boys, the Maine girls remade the beds in their room.

"While I don't mind making our bed, I do miss the housekeepers at the facility," Bells said, as she and Deanna lay their comforter over top of their sheets.

"I would rather make my own bed any day than return there," Deanna countered. "These last few days with Blake and Holly showed us just how different things really are out in the real world."

Sitting on her bed, Freya asked, "Is it really that much different?"

"Oh, you have no idea!" Deanna said, as she and Bells sat on their bed. "While we were sedated, Blake showed us memories of he and Holly growing up. He replaced them with Adam and I so we could experience it through our eyes."

"What did that look like?" Gemma asked, sitting beside Freya.

"I can see if Blake'll show you?" Deanna offered.

"Do you trust him?" Gemma asked.

"Actually, I do."

"Really?" Freya asked, eyebrows raised in surprise. "You don't trust anyone."

"Not even us some days," Bells added.

"You kind of have to see it to understand," Deanna said. "Then, they showed us trust by letting us bind and blindfold them at the facility."

"That takes a lot of trust!" Bells said, wide-eyed. "You could have easily turned them in!"

"I know. That's my point. They trusted us when they didn't have to. Holly's stronger than me. She could have easily said no, and rescued Hope on her own. However, she chose to go with the

159

plan, and rescue you guys with Adam, leaving Hope to Blake and me."

Putting her hands up in surrender, Bells said, "If you trust them, that's good enough for me." Then she sat back on the bed and smiled as she asked, "You wouldn't happen to know if those boys from Willow Bend are taken, do you?"

"Colby, the big one, is with Holly. Blake is dating Tanya," Deanna said.

"What about the other two?" Gemma asked.

Deanna chuckled. "Which ones are you guys interested in?"

Bells grinned. "Both! We've been stuck with our brothers our whole life."

"True," Deanna said, thinking about it. "I think the other two are free. You would have to ask Blake."

"I may just do that," Bells hinted.

"That's the second time you've made a point to direct us toward Blake," Freya said. "Maybe we should see if he would be willing to come in here for a little bit."

"Good idea," Deanna said, picking up the room phone.

⊕⊕⊕⊕

A FEW MINUTES LATER, there was a knock on their door. Deanna checked the peephole to see that it was Blake, so she opened the door. "Thanks for coming."

"Any time. What can I do for you ladies?" he asked, sitting on the chair at the desk of the room.

"Well, a couple things actually," Deanna started.

"Only one right now," Bells corrected. "Dee told us how you showed her your memories, but through their eyes. Could you show us too?"

"Sure," Blake said. "Lay back on your beds with your eyes closed. Hold hands with your partner on the bed with you, and then one from each will hold my hand."

On Bells and Deanna's bed, Deanna held Blake's hand, while Freya from Freya and Gemma's bed held his hand…

⊲⊳⊲⊳

"DADDY!" seven-year-old Freya shouted, running into the kitchen from outside with pig-tails in her hair. "I did it!"

Ben knelt in front of Freya and asked, "What did you do?"

"I picked up the tree. I made sure Adam checked to make sure no one was around, and I pulled the tree out of the ground!" she said, grinning ear-to-ear.

Ben threw his arms around Freya in a hug as he spun her through the air. "I'm so proud of you! Great job!"

"Want me to do it again?"

"What if we wait until tomorrow?" he asked, setting her down. "That way, you won't tire yourself out?"

"Can we make cookies instead?"

"I think that's a brilliant idea. Go get Adam and we'll make some cookies."

⊲⊳⊲⊳

"GEMMA!" Ben called. "Gemma! You and Eddie have to come in!"

After they got ready for bed, eight-year-old Gemma lay in her bed, while Ben got Eddie into bed in the same room as her since they were remodeling Eddie's room. While she lay there, she started making a story in her head.

Ben tucked them in and kissed them goodnight. As soon as he closed the door, Eddie whispered, "I like this story!"

"Thank you," Gemma said. She then used the stuffed animals to play out the story for her and Eddie.

When finished, Eddie quietly clapped. "That was great! You should write a book."

She grinned. "Someday."

"Mom's home from work," Eddie said, sensing her walk into the house.

"Shhh." Gemma turned off the lamp next to her bed.

Hope quietly came into their room. She leaned over and kissed Gemma good night. "Good night, sweetheart. Mommy's proud of you. Daddy told me your good news about what you did today."

"Thank you," Gemma whispered.

"I love you," Hope said and kissed the top of her head.

After giving Eddie a kiss goodnight as well, she left, closing the door behind her.

"Hey, Gemma?" Eddie asked.

"What?"

"Ever wonder about the others in Maine?"

"Yes. I hope they aren't being hurt."

"Me too, Gemma. Me too."

⬦⬦⬦⬦

FIVE-YEAR-OLD BELLS and Charlie were sitting at the table while Ben cooked dinner. Charlie had medium-brown hair that was longer on the top. His hazel eyes twinkled, and he always seemed to have a smile on his face.

"Bells, can you pass me the milk?" Ben asked, mashing the potatoes. "I forgot to grab it."

Charlie and Bells were frosting the sugar cookies Hope made before work. The house was already decorated for Christmas. There were presents underneath a fully decorated tree. The stockings were on the mantle with garland draped over the top of the fireplace and a fire roaring inside, blocked by the fireplace screen. There were also white lights and garland over the door-ways, adding a soft white feeling to the room.

Bells opened the refrigerator with her mind and floated the

milk to Ben. Then she closed the refrigerator with her mind.

"Thank you."

"You're welcome."

"Bells, here's a bell for you," Charlie said, passing her a bell to decorate. "I know your favorite song is *Carol of the Bells.*"

"I'm going to put my initial on it."

"Great idea!" Charlie said. "I'll put my initial on the present."

"What about mine, your mom's, and Wyatt's?" Ben asked.

"We'll make a cookie for all of us," Charlie said.

"We'll use your favorite colors," Bells added.

"I'll tell you what," Ben said, "we'll eat them tonight after dinner."

"Will Mom be home tonight?" Charlie asked.

"She and Wyatt are coming in about an hour."

"Why are her and Wyatt always together?" Charlie asked.

"Yeah. Doesn't that hurt you?" Bells asked.

"No. He's happy for her," Charlie said.

"Yes. I am happy for her," Ben explained. "She found love. You know our family is not a normal family. We love each other, but it's a different kind of love. I love your mom like a sister. You know you were both adopted. We're raising you together. She and Wyatt love each other as well. They love each other as a man and woman love each other."

"When will you find a woman to love like that?" Bells asked.

"I don't know if I ever will. However, I do know my life is full of love. I love both of you as if you were my own. I love your mom like a sister and Wyatt like a brother. We're all a family. That's all the love I need."

"We love you too, Daddy!" Bells smiled. She got up and gave him a hug.

Picking her up, he wrapped his arms around her. "You and your brother are the light in my life."

"And you are our light," Bells said.

"Daddy, are those other kids okay?" Charlie asked.

Setting Bells down, Ben and Bells went over and sat in a chair at the table with Bells on his lap. Keeping one of Bells' hands, with one of Charlie's in his other hand, Ben explained, "I wish your mom and I could have helped all of those kids. They are your brothers and sisters. Some day we may get the opportunity to help them. Until then, they are not far from our thoughts."

"How can we help them?" Bells asked.

"We can help them by making sure you are both strong enough to help when we find them," Ben explained. "All of those games we play are to make you both stronger and able to control your gifts. I am one-hundred percent certain they are getting pushed to be stronger. I wish we were the ones to teach them to use their gifts."

"Why?" Charlie asked.

"Because they would be taught to use their gifts in a way which would allow them to enjoy them, but control them at the same time. The way we use your gifts allows you to grow into your gift. They're probably getting shoved into using their gifts. I wish we could show all of them the love you are growing with. Living the way they are isn't good. It's probably scary at times."

"Whenever we get to meet them, I want to show them what love is," Bells said.

"Me too!" Charlie said. "I want to show them what we grew up with, so they know what it should have looked like."

"I agree. You two are more mature than most kids your age," Ben said. "I'm grateful for that."

⟨⊕⟨⊕⟨⊕⟨⊕

FOURTEEN-YEAR-OLD DEANNA and Adam were at the fair with Ben and Hope. Ben and Hope were getting dinner while Deanna and Adam sat at the table to save it.

"Geez," Adam grumbled.

"What?" Deanna asked.

"The minds of some of the guys around her disgust me."

"Really? What are they thinking about?"

"I don't want to tell you. I'm embarrassed to be a guy right now," he said, cheeks flushed.

"I'm sure the girls aren't too much better," Deanna pointed out.

Adam chuckled. "They're not."

"You know you can't get in their face for what they're thinking," Deanna cautioned. "Mom and Dad won't stand for that."

"Doesn't mean I have to like it. It's seriously bad."

"I don't doubt it."

"Hormone central." He rolled his eyes. "While I like these outings, I hate having to deal with the thoughts of hormonal teenagers."

Deanna laughed. "You sound like an old man!"

"No. It makes me sick to my stomach...especially when some of those thoughts are about you."

"Can't you tune it out?"

"That would be like you trying to tune out a radio on full blast. It's something I have to get used to and control. See that group of guys over there?" Adam pointed to a group of five teenage boys about their age.

"Yes."

"Their thoughts about you are not so clean."

"While you can't control their thoughts, can you control on whose thoughts you focus on?" Deanna asked.

"I can do my best. Some are louder than others."

"Focus on mine. I'll do a story for you," Deanna suggested.

"Good idea."

With that, they played one of Deanna's stories in both of their minds...even through dinner so Adam could enjoy his food.

⟨▷⟨▷◁▷◁▷⟩

Ten-year-old Freya and Charlie were playing in the woods behind the house, when Freya stopped short, staring at the ground.

"What's wrong?" Charlie asked.

"I think it's a dead bird."

"Don't touch it. I'll go get Dad," Charlie said, and ran for Ben.

Freya crouched next to the blue bird. "What happened to you, little bird?" she asked aloud. She wanted to touch it, but she did not know what killed it, so she held back. That's when she heard the baby birds in the tree above. She looked up and saw a nest. "Oh no." She frowned.

"It's right there," Charlie said, pointing to the dead bird on the ground.

"Good job not touching it," Ben said crouching next to Freya.

"Dad, there are babies in the tree above," Freya pointed out.

"Can you get the nest down here?" Ben asked.

Freya carefully levitated the nest out of the tree. A few of the twigs and some dirt fell as she lifted it off the branch where it was lodged. She kept her hands in front of her, until she gently lowered it into her hands. "There are three in here," Freya said.

"We'll feed them until they're big enough," Ben said. "In the meantime, we'll have to bury the mommy bird." He took the plastic bag out of his back pocket and wrapped the dead bird inside.

They made their way back slowly, so the babies would not be too stressed. Once back to the workshop, Ben got a box for Freya to put the birds inside. Then, while he and Charlie buried the bird, Freya watched the babies.

"Don't worry, little ones. We'll take care of you," she said, watching them chirp with their mouths open. "Just wait a few."

Ben and Charlie came back with a few worms to feed them, along with some water. Together, the trio fed and cared for the babies until they were a few months old, and strong enough to fly away.

◁▷◁▷

Fifteen-year-old Gemma and Eddie were with Wyatt, Ben, and Hope at a local rodeo. They were seated on the bleachers, watching the team roping.

"How do they do that?" Gemma asked.

"A lot of time, skill, and practice," Ben said. "It took you two a long time to sharpen your skills. It's the same for team ropers."

"What about the bull riders?" Eddie asked. "I can't imagine practice for them would be kind."

Wyatt chuckled. "No. It's not. I have a friend who is a bull rider. There isn't a bone he hasn't broken in his body."

"Why do they do it if it causes so much damage?" Gemma asked. "Why would you continuously put yourself through torture."

"Some guys do it for fame and fortune," Wyatt said with a shrug. "Some are just adrenaline junkies."

"I still don't understand. Why kill yourself for fame?"

"For some people, fame is more important than life," Hope explained. "Some people want to leave their mark on this earth. What they don't understand is that there is a miniscule amount of people who have their name written in history. It's not the fame and fortune that counts in this life. It's the lives you touch that count."

"There are times where you are blessed with a little bit of fame, while still able to help people," Wyatt said with a wink. "Being County Sherriff, there are many people who know of me. I also help people every day at work."

"Isn't your job dangerous?" Eddie asked.

"It is…but, it can also be fun. I can speed and not get a

ticket. Now, it's generally in chase, so adrenaline is added in there as well."

"There's also a chance of you not coming home," Hope pointed out.

"Yes. There's that," Wyatt agreed.

"These two are different," Eddie said knowingly, as a new team got up for their turn.

"That's Mac and Shawn. They're teens from church," Hope said. "That's probably why they feel different to you."

"Well, one is light. The other is dark," Eddie said.

"Their friend is over there," Hope pointed out Colby, standing next to the fence.

"He's really different!" Eddie pointed out.

"That's because he's a stronger Christian," Wyatt said. "I know their parents, and have watched those boys grow up. I'm afraid the rodeo life has swallowed Shawn, and Mac is struggling. Colby stepped away from riding a little bit ago, and has made some great changes in his life."

"Why?" Gemma asked.

"Because he – whoa!" Wyatt stopped mid-sentence.

On instinct, Gemma shoved Mac to the side with her telekinesis when he suddenly got bucked from the horse. A snake was in the ring, and spooked his horse while they were riding. Instead of crashing down on his leg, and possibly breaking it, he slid on the ground, and rolled, only spraining his wrist.

Ben leaned over to Gemma, and in a low voice, he reminded her, "You're not supposed to use your gift in public. I understand why you did it, but you have to be careful. Good job disguising it."

"Thank you," Gemma said, cheeks flushed in embarrassment of the reprimand. "I'm sorry."

"I know you have a tender heart. I'm just warning you to be cautious," Ben still spoke quietly. "I don't want someone seeing you, and then you getting put in some facility. I want you both to live your life to the fullest. If The Professor finds you, that won't happen. If the government figures out what the two of you can do, you'll never see the light of day. Keep it on the down-low, and never get too comfortable with your gifts."

"I will. I promise," Gemma said.

"Good girl." Ben gave her a side hug. "Now, let's enjoy the rest of the rodeo."

OPENING their eyes when the dream went black, they all four sat up, and Blake let their hands go.

"Were those real memories?" Gemma asked.

"They were," Blake assured them. "I just changed out the people, so you could associate with them better. They're real, though."

"You guys really thought about us and talked about us?" Freya asked.

"We did. We just didn't know you specifically. We knew there were more, but not how many or who you were."

"You guys weren't pushed to get your gifts stronger?" Gemma asked.

"We were challenged. There's a difference. From what I saw in Adam and Deanna's memories, Professor Roth pushed you guys beyond where you should have been at your ages. Ben challenged us and let us work up to it."

"That would be different," Bells said. "I wish I grew up the way you did."

"Here's the beauty of what we're doing," Blake explained. "You can, from this point forward, make your own choices. You won't be pushed into something you don't want to do. You can live a life with love from this point forward. Make smart choices. Make choices that will enable you to have a better future. It won't be easy. There'll be a lot of adjusting. However, Wyatt has promised you will all land in good homes with good people. We're always available to ask questions. No question is dumb. Don't be embarrassed to ask something if you need to or there's something you don't understand. Also, don't let your past be an excuse to ruin your future. Let your past fuel you to have a better future."

"I think we have a lot to think about," Deanna said.

Feeling their thoughts all over the place, Blake asked, "Want me to help sort some of that stuff out with you guys?"

"That would be great," Bells said, relieved. "Sometimes it's a lot to work sorting my own feelings, let alone feeling all of their feelings."

"I get it," Blake said knowingly. "Let's take some time to work."

◁◇◁◇◁◇▷

"THE NEXT FORTY-EIGHT hours will tell us whether she'll pull through," the doctor said to Wyatt and Holly. "I'm not going to lie. It's going to be tricky. She's currently on dialysis to get the Belladonna out of her system. We're flushing her system, as well as trying to get her back up to where she should be. She's severely dehydrated and malnutritioned. I don't know what happened to her, but I have half a mind to call the police."

Wyatt produced his badge, showing it to the doctor. "It took us a while to find her. I had to get her clear of the danger before I could bring her in. I would appreciate it if you could keep this quiet. I don't want those looking for her to find her."

"That would explain why she's listed as *Jane Doe*. I'll do my best," the doctor said. "What's her real name, so we can call her by name when she wakes up. I don't want to confuse her worse than she inevitably will be due to the trauma."

"Let me take this young lady back to the hotel, and then I'll come back here…with your permission. I really don't want Jane out of my sight until I know she'll be okay. We still have some others to find, but I want to make sure she's good first."

"I see. Is this something the FBI could help with?"

"No, sir," Wyatt said. "This is something me and my team are handling. The reach of the person in question is vast and deep. Trust is not going to be easy for us until this is over. The only reason I even stopped to bring her in is because I knew she was in bad shape and needed a hospital."

"I understand."

"I'll be back in thirty minutes. Will someone be able to let me back in?" Wyatt asked.

"Come in through here and ask for me," the doctor said, handing Wyatt a card.

"Will do. I'll be back. Thank you," he said, shaking the doctor's hand.

As Holly and Wyatt walked out to the van, Holly asked, "Do you trust that doctor?"

"I don't trust anyone right now, except Hope and you kids. That's it. I have no idea how far that man's reach extends, but if he has facilities in three different states across the country, I'm fairly confident he could find us anywhere he wanted. I'm not going to make it easy by giving them her real name or alias."

"Good idea."

"Besides, I think some downtime is a good idea for all. You all can get to know each other before we move forward to rescue the others."

Holly got in the passenger's seat, while Wyatt got in the driver's seat. After she settled and Wyatt started driving back to the hotel, Holly asked, "What's going to happen to us if Mom doesn't pull through?"

"I'll raise you. Don't worry your pretty little head. I will take care of all y'all. You kids have all been through enough, and it's only going to get worse before it gets better. I need you not to worry or lose hope."

TIME TO BREATHE

"Healing is a matter of time, but it is sometimes also a matter of opportunity." Hippocrates

*H*olly dragged her feet as she walked down the hall toward her room. She would be sharing a room with the Willow Bend girls, which had an adjoining room to the Maine girls. She felt like she was being torn between two worlds and wondered if the two would ever merge. She enjoyed her time with the Willow Bend teens over the weeks, especially with Colby and Tanya. She and Blake got close to the two of them, and the four got along great. She was curious to find out what the new teens were going to do to the dynamic of the group and what their next few weeks would look like when it came time to go rescue the two groups.

Would there, in essence, be teens scattered throughout the United States that would need to be picked up? Would Wyatt leave the Willow Bend teens here in Philadelphia with Hope, or would they go with the others in another vehicle? Carting

173

around twenty-six gifted teens and six others would be a challenge for one adult. How was Wyatt going to manage this and keep his promise? And would Hope be okay? After losing Ben, Holly was not looking forward to the prospect of losing another parent so quickly. Holly had more questions than answers. She was also exhausted, but she knew as soon as she set foot in the room, she would get bombarded with questions.

Right before she used her key card, the door to the Maine girl's room opened, and Blake walked out. Without acknowledging her, he said goodbye to the girls and closed the door. He gently grabbed Holly's arm and pulled her down near the end of the hall, where the two boy's rooms were located.

"Are you okay?" Blake whispered. "You look and feel drained."

"Good to know I look how I feel," she said, tongue-in-cheek.

Blake hugged her. She was able to hold back her emotions until that point. As soon as he hugged her, the tidal wave of emotions she was holding back, released.

She cried for a few minutes before Adam opened their door. "Come on in," he said, stepping aside to let them in.

Blake wrapped his arm around her shoulders. She allowed him to guide her into the room.

"Have a seat," Adam said, sitting on Eddie's bed with him. "I could feel you as soon as you set foot on the floor."

"Very heartbreaking and confused," Eddie elaborated.

"Yeah. Y'all telling me how I'm feeling doesn't help," Holly admitted, tucking a portion of her hair behind her ear.

"Want to get rid of some of that before you head into a room with Lindsey?" Blake asked. "I'm not so concerned with Tanya or Megan. Lindsey tends to push."

"True," Holly agreed. "I guess I'm grateful I wasn't the one to find Dad."

"I am too." Blake shuddered. "It's something I'll never

forget. However, as Mom said, she at least has the memory of knowing he's now with Jesus."

"Which brings me to another point. I'm scared for you," Holly admitted. "You are the only one in the immediate family who's not a Christian. If we head into one of the other two facilities, are you going to come out alive? We all know The Professor is still alive and is now ticked off at all of us. He's not going to let us in so easily twice. And the third facility? Ha! Chances are, it'll be in serious lockdown."

"True," Adam agreed. "We're going to need to be stealthier."

"Or, we could divide and conquer," Eddie suggested. "If we hit them simultaneously, we will have a better chance of pulling off at least one more successfully. Despite what he thinks, he's not God. He cannot be in two places at once."

"What's the chance of success on pulling them off at the same time?" Holly asked.

"A lot higher than if we did them one right after the other," Eddie pointed out.

"How would that look?" Holly asked.

"One of the Willow Bend teens drives one of the vehicles, and Wyatt drives the other," Eddie explained. "We divide our group by gifts and dive in after them."

"In other words, Bells and I are separated," Adam said. "You need at least one mind reader in each group if you're going to have a fighting chance."

"Actually, I was thinking me and you split up," Eddie said to Adam. "Bells needs to stay with the remaining Willow Bend teens. While I love her dearly, controlling emotions is not a strong enough gift to get the teens out."

"True. You and I are both strong."

"Correction, Eddie is the strongest," Holly corrected him.

"And you are the strongest telekinetic," Adam said. "So, I think she and Deanna need to be split up as well. Gemma and Freya too."

"That way, each one has two telekinetics and a mind reader," Blake said in understanding.

"What if we divide it this way?" Eddie said, logistically sorting through the groups. "Deanna, Freya, Gemma, and I go to one facility while Blake, Holly, and Adam hit the other? Freya and Gemma can help me, while Holly can help the other three. If you and Blake are both on the same team, you can stay in contact," Eddie said to Adam. "Bells can stay with the Willow Bend teens."

"Colby can drive," Holly said. "The other teens said he's the best driver from their group."

"Is Wyatt going with us, or is he staying with Mom?" Blake asked.

"He's staying here for forty-eight hours to see how she holds up. Then we're leaving her here," Holly explained.

"Is that safe?" Blake asked.

"Maybe one of the twins should stay with her here?" Adam suggested.

"That's not a bad idea," Eddie agreed. "Bells and one of the twins here, and then separate the way we've already talked about."

"Good idea," Holly said. "I would feel better if a mind reader and a telekinetic were watching over her. I don't want to leave her unguarded."

"The Willow Bend teens, except Colby, will stay here too," Eddie said.

"If they're staying, then we have to get them some games," Blake said with a smirk. "They're liable to kill each other if they don't have another outlet besides watching movies to pass their time."

"Good idea," Adam said. "Tensions are a little high with that group."

"It's not just because of boredom either," Blake added.

"No. There are some relationship issues that need to be

sorted out," Holly said in understanding. "You don't need to be a mind reader to figure that out."

"You seem to be in better spirits," Eddie observed.

"Since we have a viable plan, aren't shooting in the dark, and Mom will be looked after, I feel much better," she admitted.

"Are you ready to go in there now?" Blake asked.

"Actually, I am. Thank you guys," Holly said with a smile. "It's a huge relief to know we have a plan. I can handle the questions…mainly because I have some answers."

Eddie chuckled. "Good mindset."

"Need me to walk you to your room?" Blake asked.

"All the way to the other end of the hall?" Holly asked with a smirk. "No. I think I can handle that one. Oh! Make sure the other guys know Wyatt's not coming back here. He's staying in the hospital to watch over Mom."

"Got it," Blake said, getting up.

"See you tomorrow," Holly said as she left, closing the door behind her. She heard Blake knocking on the adjoining door as she went to her room.

Wandering down the hallway, she soaked in the fact that the others from her group were now free. She had hope.

"We were wondering when you were coming," Tanya said when Holly walked into their room.

Holly sighed as she sat down on the desk chair. "It's a lot to process, but not as much as the other group. I feel worse for them. With The Professor knowing what we're doing, it's going to be even more tricky."

"What do you mean? Do y'all have a plan?" Lindsey asked.

Holly explained the plan before they all went to bed for the night. She felt more relaxed knowing there was a viable plan in place.

❈

THE NEXT MORNING, Deanna woke up. She stretched and yawned but did her best not to wake the others.

"Dee?" Bells whispered from beside her.

"Yeah?"

"They have a plan."

"Did you hear it?"

"No. I read it. I felt Holly come in last night. Lots of anxiety, anger, frustration, and heartbreak. It was difficult not to feel her. It was like an emotional tidal wave. She got here when Blake left."

"Then what happened?"

"They talked to the boys. They plan to separate us."

"Why?"

"If they separate us, we can cover more ground," Bells explained. "They're leaving one of the twins and me with the Willow Bend teens, except Colby."

"Where's Colby going?" Deanna asked.

"Colby's going to drive one vehicle while Wyatt drives the other. You, Eddie, and the other twin are going to one facility with Wyatt, while Adam, Blake, Holly, and Colby go to the other."

"Why are they separating us?" Deanna asked. "That doesn't sound safe."

"Adam and Eddie are in agreement. It has a better chance of success if you guys hit them simultaneously," Bells explained. "The Professor can only be in one place at a time. If they hit one, he will completely lock down the other facility, and no one will get in or out. If they hit them around the same time, he won't know which one to completely lock down."

"I get it. However, my concern is the facility where he is will be a fortress."

"Just a second," Bells said, closing her eyes. In her mind, she said to Blake, *Blake? Are you awake?*

Yeah. Blake responded in her mind.

Can you have Holly come to our room? We have concerns about the plan.

Sure. Do you want me to come too? What about Adam and Eddie?

What if all three of you come? It involves all of us.

What if we all just meet together in one of the rooms? It involves everyone…including the Willow Bend group. Blake countered.

That will work. I'll get everyone up in here. What if we meet in about fifteen minutes?

Yes. I'll get the guys and meet you in your room. I'll also connect with Holly and have her and the girls with her come to your room.

Thank you.

No problem, sis.

When Blake said that, it hit Bells that Blake actually *was* her brother. He cared enough to have Charlie in the memory he shared with her. He seemed to know more about her than she cared to admit. It was strange knowing there were two more siblings in their group. What was even stranger, was knowing there were seventeen more of them!

❖❖❖❖

AFTER THEY WERE ALL GATHERED, people scattered around the room: multiple people on the beds, the couch, even sitting on the lower dresser, and the desk chair. If there was a seat anywhere, there was a teen in it.

Blake shared the plan the group of four devised the previous evening. When he finished, he said, "Bells said there was some concern."

"Is splitting us up a wise choice?" Deanna asked.

"Which one of us is staying?" Gemma asked.

Fear creased Freya's face as she grabbed Gemma's hand.

"We've never been separated in our lives."

"I know," Adam said, as Blake sent a calming feel through the room. "However, we don't have many options. We knew it would be a challenge once The Professor knew what we were up to. However, not only does he know, but he is also extremely angry with us for taking all of you, and about Deanna and I betraying him."

"That's not even mentioning the fact that Eddie hid his gifts all these years," Bells pointed out. "When he found that out, he was livid!"

"It provided the element of surprise we needed," Holly said. "I'm glad he waited."

"Thank you," Eddie said with a nod. "I knew it would come in handy at some point."

"I have to say that I'm glad to be out from under him," Gemma said. "He was a mean man."

"The worst!" Freya agreed.

"What if something happens when we're separated?" Bells asked. "How are we supposed to alert the others? Also, how are we supposed to help those in trouble, being that we will be scattered throughout the United States?"

"Honestly!" Lindsey agreed. "Megan looked it up while we waited for Tanya and Colby. I know for a fact, it's over three thousand miles between Rangeley Plantation and Corbett, Oregon. I wanted to see the distance between the facilities."

"If you calculate the distance between Philadelphia and Corbett, Oregon, and then take that away from the distance of Corbett to Creston, Wyoming, you're still talking over eighteen, almost nineteen hundred miles to get to each other if anyone needs extra help," Megan pointed out. "The distance between Creston and Philadelphia is another almost nineteen hundred miles. We're talking almost thirty hours driving straight from here to Creston. There's also about fifteen hours driving between Corbett and Creston. Once we separate, we're on our own."

Shawn huffed. "How would you know?"

"Brain? Remember? I'm a genius, idiot," Megan said, rolling her eyes.

"I thought you were the nice one," Adam said with a smirk.

"Not in the morning," Megan countered. "Especially when dealing with someone who knows better than to challenge me in the morning." Narrowing her eyes at Shawn, she added, "And he knows better."

Putting his hands up in surrender, Shawn apologized, "I'm sorry. Just seemed like odd calculations you did pretty quickly."

"Genius," Megan said sternly. "Hacker genius at that. You don't understand what you are messing with right now."

"I can understand simple math problems or even complex ones. However, pulling a distance in time and milage out of nowhere seems pretty obscure. Are you one of those people who knows a bunch of trivial stuff and just spouts off facts at random."

Megan narrowed her eyes at him. "Those weren't random. Those are specific places we were working with right now. Why would I not know them?"

"Well, I know of them, but I don't know the distances. How did you know how far they were from Philadelphia? We weren't planning on coming here?"

"I just know." She shrugged. "I'm a genius."

"What other obscure distance facts do you know? Do you know how far it is from Kalamazoo, Michigan, to Los Angeles, California?"

"About twenty-one hundred miles."

"Whoa!" Shawn's jaw dropped. "I'm impressed. What about —"

"Focus on the issue at hand," Megan snapped.

"Seriously!" Tanya sighed. "I don't think you've ever become closer to being an endangered species than you are right now."

"What did I do?" Shawn asked, stunned.

"You're an idiot every day of the week. Can't you take just one day off?" Lindsey said under her breath.

"What's that supposed to mean?" Shawn said, taken aback by Lindsey's outburst. "Why am I suddenly a target?"

"Pretty sure it's the last straw," Colby said. "You've been pushing all week. The girls are pushing back."

Shawn shoved Colby. "Some friend you are! You're supposed to be on my side!"

"Not today." Colby shook his head. "You're on your own on this one, brother. You challenged Megan."

"Why is that different than any other time I challenge people? Why is everyone ganging up on me?"

"You think you know better than everyone else," Lindsey said. "You think you know everything. You also think every girl is after you. What you don't realize is girls are smarter than you give them credit for. We tend to look below the surface."

"Not the ones I've run into."

"Really?" Lindsey crossed her arms. "And, just how many of them are you still in contact with on a daily basis?"

"Well, none," he admitted.

"Because they are not really into you. They are just after you for your status…or something else."

"Ding! Ding! Ding! Ding! Back to your corners, please?" Mac interrupted. "We've got serious life and death issues to sort through here."

"No. I seriously want to know what she meant by that!" Shawn snapped.

"No. You seriously need to shut up!" Mac snapped back.

"Not until Lindsey tells me what she meant by that."

"I neither have the time nor the crayons to explain it to you right now." Lindsey sighed. "Someone, please change the subject?"

"I want —" Shawn was cut off by an overwhelming sense that

he needed to not say a word. That was quickly followed by a peaceful feeling. "Who did that?"

"I did," Blake said. "Can we please move forward? There are people's lives at stake here."

"Fine." Shawn waved him off. "Go ahead."

"Thank you," Blake said, relieved.

"Where were we?" Eddie asked.

"The distance question," Bells reminded them. "There's danger in the distance. If a portion is here in Philadelphia, another portion are in Wyoming, and the rest are in Oregon, how are we supposed to help each other?"

"We can't," Megan said. "That was my point."

"And knowing him," Adam added, "there'll be at least one team in serious trouble. He will anticipate an attack. Even if he doesn't know where the Philadelphia group is, he certainly knows where the other two are. That means he'll be preparing for an attack on the other two facilities."

"If we give him time, he'll pit the younger ones against us," Eddie added. "Remember what he was like when we were younger?"

Bells shuddered. "Brutal."

"More like barbarous," Freya corrected.

"Do we have the forty-eight hours to wait?" Tanya asked. When everyone looked at her, she continued, "No. Seriously. Think about it. If it's about twenty-eight hundred miles to Corbett. Megan, how long was that drive?"

"Easily forty-five hours with breaks. And that's driving straight through," Megan said after a brief moment.

Shawn shook his head. "How did –?"

Lindsey turned to Shawn and said, "Your lips keep moving, but I don't know why. Have you learned nothing so far this morning?"

"Genius," Megan said again for effect. "I. Am. A. Genius."

"You're also sitting in a room full of gifted people," Freya said to Shawn. "Why do you think you guys are any less gifted in other areas? Just because you can't do what we do, doesn't mean you're not gifted."

"What you do with horses is amazing!" Mac said to Shawn. "You're like the horse whisperer."

"And, you?" Colby said to Tanya. "The things you and Megan do with computers are mind-boggling."

"What I'm saying is each of you are gifted," Freya continued. "Obviously, Megan's gift is her mind. Shawn, yours is horses. You may want to work on your personal skills, though, or you'll be living with horses for the rest of your life."

When she said that, there were several giggles heard throughout the room.

"My point," Tanya said, bringing everyone back to the conversation, "is the furthest one is almost two days of straight driving. The drivers cannot drive that. Megan, do you know the distance to the one in Wyoming?"

"That one was just south of Creston, Wyoming," Megan said. "That was about nineteen hundred miles away, or about twenty-eight or twenty-nine hours straight driving. With breaks thirty-three or thirty-four." Turning to Shawn, she narrowed her eyes and warned, "Don't ask."

"No." Shawn put his hands in the air in surrender. "I've got it now. Genius."

"You *can* teach an old dog new tricks," Lindsey said.

"Easy," Blake said. "We're all on the same team here."

Tanya went on with her thoughts, "What I'm saying is it's a long drive. The more time we give The Professor, the more time he has to prepare and the more time he has to manipulate the other groups. You said yourself he's sadistic, brutal, and barbaric," she said to Adam, Bells, and Freya. "Imagine what he's doing now that he feels threatened. Everything he's worked for over thirty, almost forty years to complete, is falling apart in front of his eyes. We don't have time to waste sitting here. This is a literal race against time."

"Agreed," Adam said. "It was good to get a good night's sleep, but we need to come up with a different plan. I understand Wyatt's heart toward Hope. Ben is gone. Hope's hanging on by a thread. We don't have time to sit for another twenty-four to thirty-six hours."

"How are we going to get to him to talk to him?" Holly asked.

"I've never done that far of a distance," Blake said, shaking his head.

"Me neither," Bells said.

"I can do it," Eddie said confidently.

"Why don't you go to the other girl's room for a little quieter area to work?" Adam suggested.

"While he does that," Colby jumped in, "why don't some of us go get breakfast for the rest of us. This thinking on an empty stomach is not a good thing."

"That sounds like a great idea," Adam agreed.

"Since there are cameras, we don't want you guys to be caught," Megan said to the Maine teens. "We should be the ones to go."

"I'll go," Tanya volunteered.

"Me too," Colby said.

"I will, too," Megan said.

"I'll go too," Mac volunteered.

"Sounds like a plan," Adam said. "The rest of us will just stay in here."

⟨▸⟨▸⟨▸⟨▸

EDDIE WHEELED into the other room and fixed the breaks of his chair once he settled. He hid his gifts for so long that he hoped they would work as well as he thought. When he cut loose with his telekinesis, he was stronger than he thought. He hoped the same would happen regarding mind connections.

He closed his eyes and cleared his thoughts. He pictured Wyatt in his mind until he saw him in Hope's hospital room, holding her hand, praying. *Wyatt?*

Wyatt looked around the room. The hair on the back of his neck stood on end. "Who's there?" he asked aloud.

Wyatt, this is Eddie. I'm at the hotel.

"How are you doing that?" Wyatt asked.

Shhh! No one can hear me except you.

"You're literally in my mind?" Wyatt asked, wide-eyed. He gulped as he looked around to see if anyone saw him talking to himself.

Yes. Now stop talking out loud. People will think you're crazy.

Good point, Wyatt thought.

Good. There ya go. Listen, all of us teens have been talking, and we want to include you in everything. We have some concerns…

As Eddie explained what was going on, Wyatt understood. He was torn between wanting to be there for Hope and getting to the others quickly. The teens were right. There was no time to waste. The longer they stayed, the more time The Professor had to prepare. He did not want to give The Professor an even bigger advantage than he already had right now.

Y'all are right. I'll come get whichever twin is staying here and Bells. Tell them not to worry. I'll show them how to use the cafeteria and vending machines, as well as give them money for a few weeks. I'll keep the teens checked into the hotel for when the others need a break, Wyatt explained. *Have those coming here get ready. I'll be there in about twenty minutes. Tell the others to get ready as well. We leave in an hour.*

TIME TO HIT THE ROAD

"We must use time as a tool, not as a crutch." John F. Kennedy

*A*fter getting everyone settled and buying the Willow Bend teens some games and snacks, Wyatt and Colby left to buy another van and autonomous GPS.

When they returned, Colby took off with Holly, Blake, and Adam for the facility south of Creston, Wyoming in the new van, leaving the one with bullet holes to Wyatt. They decided he could show his badge if they got pulled over. They also taped the broken window closed with clear plastic and duct tape. That way, it would cut some of the cold from coming into the van.

The group Colby, Holly, Blake, and Adam were going to rescue were ten-year-olds. Their trip would be a good thirty to thirty-five hours. Meanwhile, Wyatt took off with Deanna, Freya, and Eddie for Corbett, Oregon, the facility for the thirteen-year-olds. It would be a forty-three-hour drive.

⟨⟩⟨⟩⟨⟩⟨⟩

"Do you think they'll be okay so far away from everyone?" Megan asked.

"I think I'm glad Blake and Holly are together and with Colby," Tanya said. "I know they'll look after and protect Colby. Wyatt can handle himself."

"Do you think they'll succeed?" Mac asked as the group was playing Texas Hold 'em, with little candies as their pot. They moved the desk in the girl's room between the beds, with a chair at both ends. Some were on the beds and some in the chairs.

"I think we need to pray…a lot," Shawn said, flipping the first three cards.

"Ouch!" Megan cringed. "I'm out."

"We haven't even bet yet," Mac objected.

"I'm can't even with this hand. Who dealt this mess anyway?" Megan asked.

"I did," Shawn said.

"You need to learn to shuffle better. These are horrible," Megan said, laying her cards on the table facedown.

"How do you know the other cards won't help you?" Shawn asked.

"Because I would have a greater chance of draining the Mississippi with a straw than winning this hand," Megan said. "It's really bad."

"How do you know?"

"Do I have to say it again?" Megan rolled her eyes. "Let me spell it out for you: G-e-n-i-u-s. I am a genius."

"All right. You don't have to hit me in the head with a frying pan."

"Maybe a hockey stick because I've said it no less than three times alone today," Megan said to Shawn. "I'm mean really, you're not seriously that dense, are you?"

"No. I just…sometimes I don't understand how you do so

much in your head." Holding his hand up to stop her, Shawn added, "I don't need reminded, just clarifying."

"Fair enough," Megan said. "At times like this, I wish we could be online."

"Not going to happen until they're back," Mac said. "And, check."

The others checked, so Shawn flipped the next card.

"I'm going to play three," Mac said, putting three pieces of candy in the middle.

"I'll match that," Tanya said, putting her three in.

Shawn added his three, as did Lindsey. "Ready?" Shawn asked. When everyone nodded, he flipped over the last card.

"Thank you!" Mac said, adding five more.

"I'm out," Tanya said, laying her cards face down.

Lindsey laid her cards face down as well. "I'm out too."

Mac looked at Shawn, who was studying him. "Well?" Mac asked.

Shawn cocked his head to the side. "Call," he said, tossing in five pieces of candy. When Mac clicked his tongue, Shawn said, "Show 'em."

"You won," Mac grumbled. "You know me too well."

"I do," Shawn said, sliding all the candy to his pile.

While Mac collected the cards and shuffled them, Megan got up and grabbed a soda from the refrigerator. "Anyone want anything?"

"A little early for that. Isn't it?" Mac asked.

"It's my vice," she said, opening the soda, taking a swig. "Ahhh," she said when she finished. "Caffeine will infuse into my system momentarily. Okay, Mac, let's see what you can do."

❖❖❖❖

AFTER A FEW HOURS OF PLAYING, Shawn's pile was considerably larger than everyone else's pile of candy.

"I think I've figured out another one of your gifts," Tanya said, tossing her cards to the side. "Fold."

"He's good at playing cards," Mac said.

"Does that mean he's good at calling people's bluff?" Megan asked.

"More like I know when someone's lying," Shawn said and then looked pointedly at Lindsey.

"Why are you looking at me?" Lindsey asked, wide-eyed.

"Because you have a nasty habit of lying about your feelings," Shawn said. Then he threw three pieces of candy into the pot. "Raise."

As the others added to the pot, Lindsey asked, "What do you mean?"

"I know when you like someone. You try to play it off or make yourself seem like someone you're not to impress them."

"And you don't?" Lindsey challenged.

"Enough!" Tanya said. Slamming her cards down, she looked pointedly at Shawn and Lindsey. "This is going to be torture if you two don't talk out your feelings. You have two choices: do it here, or go to the other room and talk."

"Are you serious?" Lindsey asked, appalled.

"Those are your choices. Avoiding it is over. We don't have the comfort of separating you two for the duration of this."

"You are serious?" Lindsey asked, stunned.

"You have ten seconds to make your choice before I start the conversation right here," Tanya warned.

Shawn shook his head. "You can't make us talk."

"Shawn, you once told me –"

"Stop right there, shortcake!" Shawn cut Tanya off.

"I am both of your confidants," Tanya said. "I will make you both talk."

"I give," Shawn said, putting his hands up in surrender. "Here or our room?" Shawn asked Lindsey.

"Your room," she mumbled, getting up from her spot between Mac and Megan.

When they left the room, they closed one of the doors between the rooms.

"I would love to be a fly on the wall during that conversation!" Megan smirked.

"It's only a conversation at least three years in the making," Mac said. "It's about time."

"Yes," Tanya said, looking directly at Megan and Mac. "Let's not wait that long for you two."

"What does that mean?" Mac asked, fear in his eyes.

"I've seen the way you look at Megan. Megan, I know how you feel. I can't be your best friend and not notice. It's time you two had a conversation too."

⬦⬦⬦⬦

"WELL?" Lindsey asked, sitting on what used to be Colby's bed. It was now Mac's until Colby returned.

Sitting on the edge of his bed, Shawn intertwined his fingers and sighed. "I don't know how we're supposed to start this."

"Fine," Lindsey huffed. "Yes. I have liked you since we were kids. However, over the last few years, I've seen you slipping further and further down the rabbit hole."

"What does that mean?"

"You're following the path of those famous rodeo riders you're so fond of. Going rodeo to rodeo…girl to girl…leaving broken hearts all over the country."

"Like you don't do that in school? I've seen you go from guy to guy…heck, school to school!"

"Put the boxing gloves down," Tanya said, walking into the room.

"What are you doing in here?" Shawn asked.

As she sat on the bed beside Lindsey, she explained, "You two need a referee for your conversation. The other two don't."

"Really?" Shawn asked, eyes wide. "Mac and Megan?"

"You really are dense!" Lindsey shot. "She's liked him for a long time."

"Girls," Shawn huffed, shaking his head, crossing his arms.

"Work with me, people!" Tanya snapped. "Let's take this one step at a time. Shawn, tell me what you like about Lindsey?"

⟨⟩⟨⟩⟨⟩

"So," Mac said, after Tanya left the room, "want to tell me something?"

"Not really," Megan said. "I was hoping to save this for another conversation. However, Tanya's right. We'll all kill each other if we don't get this stuff out."

Mac grinned. "Do you really like me?"

Looking at him out of the corner of her eye, she admitted, "I used to. There are times I do see the Mac I used to like."

"I don't understand."

"When the three of you started going to the rodeos without your parents, I watched all three of you slide off the path," Megan explained. "Then, I saw what you two did to Colby when he fought his way back. He made the changes necessary to get back to Christ, and you both ridiculed him relentlessly!"

"We did." His face flushed. "I know it was wrong. I didn't want to lose my friend."

"We've already had that conversation," Megan pointed out.

"We did. And, I've done a lot of thinking since then. I know it seems like it was a long time ago, but in reality, it wasn't all that long ago."

"But –"

"Please?" Mac asked, cutting her off. When she covered her mouth, he continued, "I've watched you over the years, more

192

closely over the last few days. I've seen your Bible beside your bed. You are basically hiding for your life, and you still thought to not only bring your Bible but also to take time to be with God."

"You didn't?" Megan asked, surprised.

"Did the other girls?"

"Of course. We take time after breakfast. We've even started reading a Proverbs per day aloud during breakfast and talking about it while we eat."

"Man! I wish we did that!" Mac said. "Colby brought his but keeps to himself. I know," he said, putting his hands up to stop Megan from talking. "I know we made him feel that way by making fun of him. He's a strong guy inside and out. Holly has a good one."

"Mac, you're a good one too. You're just a bit confused right now."

"Right. And, I don't want to be. Whether we end up dating or not – not that I'm asking right now, mind you," Mac stammered. "However, even if we don't, I still want to be sure to do right by the Lord. This treading water, hoping nothing happens to me, is getting old."

Megan thought for a moment before she responded. It was almost too long for Mac. "Mac, if you want to join us in the mornings, we would love to have you over. I'm sorry you're put in the position you're currently in, but you do need to make a choice. Do you want to live for and worship the Lord or Shawn?"

"Wow! Nothing like cutting to the core."

"There's no more dancing around it, Mac," Megan said. "You need to make a choice. You're standing at the crossroads. It may cost you your friend, but you'll gain so much more!"

"I know."

"You know in your head, but you're still struggling in your heart."

"Dang! How did you get so smart?"

"Genius, remember," she said with a smile.

"You are not only book smart but heart-smart too. That's a rare combination."

Megan blushed. "Thank you."

Mac chuckled. "I honestly don't know too many people who can go toe-to-toe with Shawn. I know even less who could do it and win. You do. You're stronger than you think you are."

"Confidence and God. I know when I stand up, I'm doing it with the right intentions. There are times, I will admit, that I'm just really tired and he's stepped on my last nerve. However, I do try not to let that happen."

"I hear ya," Mac chuckled again, shaking his head. "Meg, I really do like you."

"I like you too, but I need you to do whatever changes and choices you need to do for yourself and to get right with God. I would be happy to help, with no strings attached. If we decide later we have a brother/sister relationship, then so be it."

"If we decide we want to date later, is that still an option?" Mac asked.

"I think we'll cross that bridge when we get to it. Again, I want you to do whatever you're going to do for you and God, not me and you. You need to be healthy in order to be in a healthy relationship."

"I am healthy."

"No. You're co-dependent. You depend on Shawn for your friends and choices. You need to depend on Jesus."

"Fair enough. Agreed," Mac said, sticking his hand out.

Megan glanced down at his hand and shook her head. She wrapped her arms around him in a hug instead.

"Thank you."

"No. Refocus. Thank God."

⟨⊳⟨⊳⟨⊳⟨⊳

"WE HAVE time to sort this out," Shawn said. "Why do we need to do this right now?"

"You can use time as a tool or crutch," Tanya said. "We're going to use this time constructively. Now, I have a lot on both of you. I would rather not use it. I would rather the two of you have a deep conversation without boxing gloves. If you can't, I'll use all the ammunition I have in my arsenal. So, Shawn, what do you like about Lindsey?"

"Well, I think she's pretty."

Lindsey clicked her tongue.

"What's that for?" Shawn asked, taken aback. "That's a compliment."

"If Holly asked you why you liked her, what would you say?" Lindsey asked.

"She's strong, confident, and pretty."

"So, you like her for more than her looks?" Lindsey asked.

"Definitely!"

"Why do you only like me for my looks?"

"Who said I did?"

"Why was it the first and only thing you said?" Lindsey challenged.

Shawn sighed. Rubbing his temples, he closed his eyes for a moment and took a deep breath. Slowly letting it out, he glanced from Tanya to Lindsey before landing back on Tanya. "Is there some way I can have an interpreter? I feel like whatever I say is going to get twisted."

"I can understand that," Tanya agreed. "Let's try this my way." She grabbed a pillow off the bed. "Whoever is holding this is the only one who can talk or make noise. In other words, no comments from the peanut gallery. Yes, Lindsey, that means you. Let him talk," she said and then passed the pillow to Shawn.

"You didn't let me finish," Shawn said. "I do think you're pretty. I also think you're smarter than you give yourself credit for. Please don't take how I say this the wrong way?" he asked

Lindsey. "Please let me finish to clear it before you jump?" When she nodded, he continued, "You can take situations and manipulate them to come out how you want them to. It's like when I play Texas Hold 'em. I can manipulate the game. You can manipulate people. You have a gift of knowing just what someone needs to hear or get in order for you to get what you want. That's actually a good thing. Well, it can be used for good or bad. You've studied people for so long, you know what makes them tick."

"I'm honestly not sure how to take that."

"Take it as a compliment and be quiet," Tanya said, and then nodded for Shawn to go on.

"You exude confidence. While Holly is confident and strong, you are in a different way. If you could harness that and use it for good and not evil, it would almost be your superpower!"

"Okay, not really sure if we're getting better, but go on," Lindsey said.

"I know I'm saying this wrong. I admire that skill in you. I know you're a Christian. If you could focus that gift on forwarding the Kingdom, Satan will be running from Willow Bend with his tail between his legs. If you would focus more on the Kingdom and less on guys and cheerleading, can you imagine what you could do?"

Lindsey looked to Tanya with her hands out.

Tanya took the pillow from Shawn and gave it to Lindsey. "Same rules," she warned Shawn. He only nodded in response.

"What you just said to me could be applied to you ten-fold. You go to a rodeo, and after every rodeo, I hear through the school about the two or three girls you had during that rodeo."

Shawn's face flushed the brightest shade of red Tanya ever saw.

"Are you a virgin?" Lindsey asked.

"I-I don't think that's a question I want to answer," Shawn

said, appalled. "I don't think that's a question I should have to answer."

"Why not?" Lindsey asked.

"Are you?" he challenged.

"I-I –"

"Yeah. Sucks. Doesn't it?"

"I am," Lindsey admitted. "I know my reputation doesn't seem that way, but I am a virgin. I have done other things I am ashamed to admit."

"Are you –"

"Lindsey!" Tanya said, eyes wide, cutting Shawn off.

"We never actually did it. The guys said they would tell their friends we did it just to keep their reputation," Lindsey explained. "So, I let them."

"But it ruined yours!" Shawn shot.

"What about yours?" Lindsey asked tears in her eyes. "How many girls exactly have you *had*?"

"I, well, I…" his voice faded.

Lindsey gasped. "You're not a virgin. Are you?"

Shawn reluctantly shook his head.

"And you're preaching at me on how to be a good witness for the Kingdom!" Lindsey stood, her hands clenching the pillow. "You have some nerve! I never ever want to talk to you again!" she shouted through her tears. She threw the pillow at Shawn's head. He ducked, the pillow narrowly missing his head as she went toward the door. Hand on the handle, she turned toward Shawn and said, "You will never know what it's like to feel me love you. You have ruined ever having your wife be your first and only! That's a gift you can never get back! You have no idea how much I hate you right now!" she said and left into the room with Mac and Megan.

"Tanya, I…" Shawn's voice faded as he shook his head.

"I don't even want to know how many," Tanya said, equally in shock. "I never thought you would honestly cross that line.

That's a line God made perfectly clear. Maybe you should sit in here and have a one-on-one with God," she suggested. "I'm not judging. I'm imagining how many times you broke Jesus's heart over the years."

"There's no way to get it back."

Tanya shook her head. "There really isn't."

Mac walked into the room. He glanced back at Megan, who was holding a sobbing Lindsey, before he shut the door. He went over to the chair at the desk and sat down. "What's going on? We can't get much out of Lindsey."

"I hurt her more deeply than I ever thought I could," Shawn admitted.

Narrowing his eyes, he demanded, "What did you do?"

"I admitted I wasn't a virgin," Shawn mumbled.

Mac grabbed Shawn by his collar and picked him up off the bed. Despite their size difference, Mac got into Shawn's face. Shawn looked beat up as it was, so he let Mac do what he wished he could do to himself.

"How dare you hurt her like that! I thought you did things with those girls, but never this!"

"The pressure was intense!" Shawn said, begging for him to understand. "The pressure at school was just as bad!"

Mac jerked Shawn toward him before he threw him to the bed. "I can't even," he said, and left for the other room.

"That went well," Tanya said in a sigh when the door slammed behind Mac. "Just be grateful Colby or Blake aren't here."

"Yeah. That would not have gone well," Shawn admitted, not getting off the bed from where Mac threw him.

Tanya got up and went over to his bed. When he sat up, she hugged him. "I know you can't fix this. There's no getting it back. I also know you're standing at a crossroads." Letting him go, she continued, "Do you want to keep going down the path you're on, or do you want to come back to Christ? You can't have it both ways."

Tears slowly fell onto his cheeks as he shook his head. "I'm not worthy. I've messed up so bad. There's no turning back now."

"You're kidding, right?"

"Everyone is ticked off at me."

"Because they know you ruined yourself."

"Gee. Thanks."

"You know what I mean. That anger is manifested from severe hurt. Lindsey really liked you. You really did ruin that one. Mac and Megan are not happy with you for hurting her and yourself."

"I didn't hurt myself."

"Are you sure?" Tanya challenged.

"What do you mean?"

"You had one gift to give your wife that you would never be able to give anyone else. Every time you have sex, you give a part of yourself to that girl. I'll bet you probably don't even remember their names," she challenged.

"No. Not really."

"I've watched you grow colder through the years, and now I know why."

"How can I fix this?"

"Well, I think that starts with you and God. I'll stand beside you and walk with you if you want to make those changes. If you choose to continue down the path you're going on, you may gain more women fans and the admiration of the guys at school, but you'll lose those who truly care for your heart and soul. Think of the story of the prodigal son. He gained a lot of fame while he had his inheritance. What happened when that was gone?"

"He was alone and ate pig slop."

Tanya slapped the back of his head.

"What's that for?" he asked, rubbing the back of his head.

"You know the stories! You know the parables! Why did you throw your pearls before swine?"

Shawn sighed. "I know. I suck!"

Tanya went over and pulled the Bible from the drawer. She looked up Luke 15:11-32, and handed it to Shawn. "Read this. Take some time with God. I'll be next door picking up the pieces of Lindsey. Let me know when you're done. I think you need the time alone."

"I think you're right."

❖❖❖❖

HOLLY SAT in the passenger's seat, with Blake and Adam in the second seat while Colby drove. "This is weird," Holly said after a few hours of them talking and driving. "I was nervous when we headed toward Maine, but this is on a different level. We know The Professor knows we're on the way. We actually have less power, but we have more to rescue."

"We also have a lot more unknowns," Adam added. "We have the schematics to study on the way there, but we don't know for sure what the facility is like. We don't know what the kids are like. We had a lot of advantages in Maine we won't have with the other two facilities."

"We'll need a lot more prayer," Holly said decisively. "We not only have to pray for us, but also for the other groups. We don't know if The Professor knows where Mom is or not. If he does, does he know where the Willow Bend teens are? If he does, is he going to leave them alone or use them against us?"

"So many questions," Adam said.

"With no answers," Blake added.

"So, I've been thinking," Colby said, "you know, since we had nothing but time while y'all were in Maine."

"Yes?" Holly asked.

"We have about a day to figure out our game plan here in

Wyoming. Afterward, our plan is to get out of town. Are we going to wait until the other group is in Oregon, or are we going to guess and hope for the best on when to hit the facility? And what if we run into The Professor again? Are you going to be the one to stop him, Holly? If so, what does that look like?"

"Wow!" Blakes eyebrows arched in surprise. "You have been thinking!"

"Not only that," Colby continued, "but also regarding your eternal security, Blake? I know you said you wanted to wait until this is over. Tanya and I talked about it while we were going through Ben's workshop. With oh so many questions looming, are you really willing to gamble with your eternal security? Are you really willing to wait until this is over to sort that out? What happens if you don't make it out alive? You have a defensive gift, not an offensive gift. Holly is honestly the only one in this group with an offensive gift. I'm not exactly sure why we sent three telekinetics one direction and only brought one with us?"

"Because the other group is going after the next oldest group – the thirteen-year-olds," Holly explained. "If Professor Roth will be anywhere, we're pretty sure that's where he's headed."

"What makes you say that?" Colby asked. "This is basically our lives that you're gambling on with this theory."

"He has more to lose with the older group," Adam explained. "There are only eight ten-year-olds. There are nine thirteen-year-olds. He has also invested more time with that group. If he loses them, he loses the traction he had with our group and the Oregon group. Knowing him the way I do after studying those files, I'm ninety-nine-point-nine percent certain he's going to Oregon. He'll also feel more protected with the older gifted ones."

"And yes, my gift is defensive. If you remember, I can compel other to do things if need be," Blake reminded him. "That's why I was sent with these two."

"True," Colby said, considering Adam's words. "I didn't

think of it that way. Good points. What about what I asked you, Blake?"

"What?" Blake asked.

"You didn't answer my concern about you. There's no avoiding it. We're going to be on the road another twenty-six hours."

"I know," Blake said, leaning forward, interlacing his fingers together. "I also know it's a difficult decision."

"Why is it a difficult decision?" Adam asked.

"Because I'll be giving my life in service to Jesus. Basically, handing over my life to His will."

"And?" Adam pressed.

"And what? Are you a Christian?"

"I've prayed and asked Christ to guide and direct my life and to forgive me of my sins…yes," Adam declared. Turning toward Holly, he admitted, "I may have taken a few strolls through yours and Wyatt's minds to gather the facts necessary to make an informed decision."

"If your decision was *yes*, I don't care how you got the information," Holly said with a smile. "I'm just glad to call you a brother here on earth and in Christ. What about you, brother?" she asked Blake.

Blake shook his head. "I still don't know."

"May I ask what's holding you back?" Colby asked.

"A lot, actually," Blake admitted. "This whole situation, for instance. Why would a God of love let that man get away with all he's gotten away with? He killed our mothers and killed Ben. I can't imagine who else he had killed over the years. I'm sure there were more."

"I would counter with the fact that God provided Adam and Deanna to help everyone get out," Colby said as he continued to focus on driving. "Y'all didn't get to Ben in time to save his life, but Hope had the time to save his soul. The Lord also gave Ben and Hope the strength to take you two in the first place, and

Wyatt the wisdom on how to handle the entire situation. It's all in how you look at it. You can find His hands guiding and directing, or you can see the bad."

"How is The Professor still walking this earth?" Blake asked. "He's pure evil."

"Free will," Colby explained. "God doesn't want us to be puppets, doing His bidding. He wanted us to choose to follow Him to begin with. And then continue to choose to follow and worship Him daily. That free will has another side, though. That free will allows The Professor to choose death and destruction as well."

"How is that fair?"

"God never said life on this earth would be fair," Colby countered. "He just said He would be with us every step of the way. He provided us salvation through Jesus Christ's example. Jesus provided the sacrifice, allowing us the honor of eternal security in Heaven with Him when we die. Until then, if you are a follower of Christ, He walks with you every day, facing whatever you have to face. You're never alone. He also provided a guide in the Holy Spirit. The Spirit helps us stay focused on the path God has for us."

"And if you're not one of His?" Blake asked.

"Then you're one of Satan's…pure and simple."

"I see. So, you're saying right now –"

"That you belong to Satan," Colby cut him off. "Yes."

"Oh!"

"Perspectives, my man. Perspectives."

⸎⸎⸎⸎

"Okay, while we drive, we need to make a viable plan," Wyatt said to his group.

Deanna sat in the passenger's seat, while Freya and Eddie sat in the second seat, with Eddie's chair beside him in the open area normally used for those going to the back of the van.

"Can we make a viable plan?" Eddie asked.

"We can make a semi-viable plan," Wyatt countered. "The plan will never go exactly according to plan, but we can at least make a valiant effort. It needs to stay fluid."

"With The Professor knowing we're coming, what can we do?" Freya asked.

"Yeah. We can't just walk in like we did in Maine," Deanna added.

"You're right. You can't," Wyatt agreed. "So, think of another option. Don't give me what you can't do, but what you can do."

"Can we see the pictures the others took?" Deanna asked.

"Megan's computer is in the bag between the seats. She took the passcode off so y'all could access the information," Wyatt explained.

Freya reached forward and pulled the computer out of the bag. Booting it up, she easily found the folder with the photos Colby and Tanya took. While she was in there, she found the pictures of the files of their mothers. As soon as she opened the file, she gasped.

"What?" Deanna asked.

With tears in her eyes, she said, "The pictures of our mothers."

Eddie leaned over and looked at the computer. He hit the down arrow to scroll through the photos. "This is mine," he said. Choking back the tears, he added, "It says her name was Erin Taylor."

"Ours was Serina Dalton. We looked a lot like her, but these photos are…" She shook her head.

"Brutal. I know," Deanna said, cutting her off. "We looked at them on the way to Maine in the folder Blake brought with him."

"Why did he do this?" Freya asked, tears in her eyes.

"With your mothers gone, he would have complete control over you," Wyatt explained. "If your mothers were still around, pretty sure they would object to your treatment."

"This one's Charlie's," Eddie pointed her out to Freya. "It says her name was Cara Gombeda. Looking at their before pictures, I can't help but notice how beautiful they all were."

"We did, too," Wyatt agreed. "It's like he handpicked women who were natural beauties."

"He definitely had a type," Freya said.

"Have you found the schematics yet?" Wyatt asked, changing the subject.

"They're right here," Freya said, opening the folder.

"This is Maine, this is Wyoming, and this is Oregon," Eddie pointed them out. They printed the Wyoming facility for them on the hotel's printer, leaving the computer to the other group.

Pulling up Oregon's facility, Freya whistled. "This is huge."

"Does it say where the kids are being held?" Wyatt asked.

"I'll bet they're on this level," Eddie pointed to the fifth picture. "This one is five levels tall. If he follows suit, the dorm floor will be on the top level. It's a little difficult to scale five levels."

"Not for a telekinetic," Freya said with a wink.

"True," Eddie agreed.

"No disrespect, but how are you going to get up five floors?" Wyatt asked Eddie. "I can see the other two, but you will have a different set of challenges."

"I will. It's not disrespectful to acknowledge I have limits," Eddie said. "However, I am also telekinetic. I can get myself up the five levels. We can all get ourselves up that high. It's what we do when we get there that'll make the difference."

"Fair enough," Wyatt said. "Then, we'll talk general. How are y'all going to get past the guards who I'm sure The Professor already has everywhere?"

"However, we have to," Deanna said sternly. "We will get them out, whatever it takes."

"What if that means you have to kill someone?" Wyatt asked. "Are you ready to do that?"

"We'll do whatever it takes," Deanna said forcefully.

"Just do me a favor, and do your best not to kill anyone?" Wyatt asked.

"They didn't think twice when they killed Ben and almost killed Hope," Deanna countered.

"When we were in the hotel, Blake put some of his and Holly's memories in our minds," Freya said. "He replaced themselves with some of us, so we would feel what they did. Seeing Ben the way Blake and Holly did, makes me feel like I lost my own dad."

"I agree," Deanna said. "We had more because of what he showed us in the hospital."

"I wish I could have felt those," Eddie said. "The Professor is my only example of a dad."

"I promise you that is not an example of a dad," Wyatt objected. "A dad loves, guides, and directs. When he has to, he puts his foot down. However, a dad should never throw you in a room and lock you in or use your siblings against you. That's not a dad. That's a tyrant!"

"You seem very passionate about this," Eddie observed.

"I helped raise Blake and Holly," Wyatt explained. "I took care of them when they were sick. I helped train them. I helped look after them. To the rest of the world, I just looked like a close friend of the family. To the family, they knew Hope and I were together, and the kids looked at me like a bonus dad. They are just as much my kids as they are Hope's and were Ben's. They are our children in heart and love. Blood doesn't make you family…loyalty does."

"That's a strong statement," Deanna said, surprised.

"When you run into your other siblings, something you have

to remember is they have no idea who you are. Remember the feeling you had when you met Blake and Holly?" Wyatt asked Deanna.

"Yes."

"Remember how you struggled to look at them as your brother and sister?"

"Yes."

"When you first meet this group in Oregon, it's going to be the same thing. You're going to have to figure out a way to quickly get them to trust you," Wyatt said. "Do you have a plan for that?"

"I hadn't thought of that," Deanna admitted.

"You're going to have to fight the guards. You're going to have to fight your siblings to rescue them. And, you may even have to fight The Professor…again."

"Trust me. I have The Professor covered," Eddie said. "He and I have some unfinished business."

"I bet!" Wyatt said in a chuckle.

"That man made me watch as he pushed Charlie to the point of killing him. He made me watch as he pushed my brothers and sisters beyond where they should have been pushed. He used my brothers and sisters against each other. If he ever had a clue as to what I could do, I promise you I would have been his pet project."

"I'm sure you would have. If you're as strong as I think you are, you are the strongest of the bunch. You have some serious skills!" Deanna remarked. "Your telekinesis is stronger. You contacted Wyatt from miles away at the hospital, which means you're stronger than Adam or Blake."

"Yeah." Wyatt chuckled. "That was wild!"

"I'm just glad I was able to reach you," Eddie said. "I honestly wasn't sure if I could."

"I'll bet you're even stronger than you think," Deanna said.

"And I have a feeling we're going to need that strength when we get to Oregon."

"I know," Eddie agreed. "Knowing him the way I do, with the gift I have for calculating the future, I'm pretty sure that's where he's heading. If I had to place a bet, it would be there. He's already killed Ben, and Hope took a really good hit. The Willow Bend teens are currently out of the picture, so he's not looking for them. Wyatt helped lead four of his strongest in Adam, Deanna, Blake, and Holly in taking the rest of us from him. He's out for vengeance."

"Is there any way of you knowing where he actually is?" Deanna asked.

"Not at this distance. I'm good, but I'm not that good. I could only follow you and Adam when you left to the border of Maine."

"What do you mean?" Deanna asked.

"I was able to follow you and Adam when you left the facility for Texas. It was a game I used to play. I would pick someone and follow them off the campus as they went home," Eddie explained. "When The Professor sent you and Adam away, I wanted to know where you were going, so I followed you with my mind. I was connected to you until you crossed into Massachusetts."

"I have to admit," Wyatt said, "that's impressive. Can you connect with the other van right now?"

"Actually, I think I can. I can use Blake or Adam to boost," Eddie said. "Is there something you want me to find out?"

"Maybe find out if they're staying the night somewhere?"

"Just a second," Eddie said, closing his eyes. He had to search to find them. While they took off about the same time, their van traveled faster than the other one, so it left them a while back.

Adam? Eddie thought.

Yeah? Adam asked.

Are you guys staying the night anywhere?

Just a second, Adam thought. A moment later, Adam responded in his mind, *No. They want to get there as soon as possible.*

Thank you.

No problem. Be careful, Adam warned *I've done the calculations. He's going to be in Oregon.*

I agree. That doesn't mean Wyoming will be easy by any means.

No. That just means The Professor won't be there to create more havoc. Eddie, do what you have to do to rescue the others.

They will get out. I give you my word.

Thank you. I looked at the files, Adam thought. *Those are our brothers and sisters. We want to give them a different life than we've had so far.*

Agreed.

Good luck.

You too, Eddie thought. Then he opened his eyes and explained, "No. They're driving through."

"Then we need to as well," Wyatt said, "They're going to Wyoming. That's at least fourteen or fifteen hours before we hit Oregon. As soon as they get a head's up that Wyoming is hit, they'll double their efforts on Oregon."

"Not if we ask Wyoming to wait for fifteen hours?" Deanna suggested. "We'll push, but if we can hit Oregon before they get Wyoming or at the same time, then they won't have a head's up."

"Eddie?" Wyatt asked, glancing in the rearview mirror at Eddie.

Eddie closed his eyes again. *Adam?*

Yeah?

Can you guys hold off for about fifteen hours? We don't want to warn Oregon that we're on the way. If we can either hit them the same time or close to the same time, they won't have enough time to know for sure which one we're going to hit.

Just a second, Adam thought. Then he cleared his throat, "That's Eddie again. He wants to know if we'll hold off our end of things for about fifteen hours."

"Why?" Colby asked.

"Because that'll give Oregon notice that they're coming. They'll fortify even stronger than they already are if we trigger the alert in Wyoming first."

"I think that's a fair request," Colby said, mulling over Adam's words. "What do y'all think?"

"I think it's fair," Blake said. "They'll have a better shot at it if they hit before or at the same time we do."

"What if we set a time?" Holly asked. "If they trigger it first, Oregon will alert Wyoming, and it will be trickier for us."

"Good point," Colby agreed.

Thinking through the two timelines, Holly suggested, "We targeted Maine in the morning. They'll be expecting that. What if we target the two facilities around dinner time? Say about five-thirty on Thursday night?"

"I like that idea," Adam agreed. "Most people are on their break at that time. They'll be expecting something in the morning or when it's dark."

"That'll give us time to figure out how to access the facilities," Holly said. "We can't go in the same way."

"Good thinking, sis," Blake agreed.

"Okay," Adam said. Taking a few moments, he reconnected with Eddie. *Are you there?*

Yes. I've been hanging out, waiting for you to get back. I wasn't sure if you could get back with me.

I doubt it. The further we get apart, the less chance I have of connecting, Adam thought.

What did you guys decide? Eddie thought.

What if we both breach the facilities at five-thirty on Thursday night Wyoming time?

Eddie calculated the time and distance in his mind before he responded, *That'll work. That'll be six-thirty Oregon time. Wyoming is on mountain time.*

That sounds accurate, Adam confirmed.

Agreed. Six-thirty our time, five-thirty your time on Thursday night.

Perfect. We'll take at least one night sleeping in the van so Colby can get some rest.

We can't if we're going to make it on time. Good luck, brother.

Good luck to you too! Adam said and cut the connection.

"It's agreed," Eddie said. "We'll both breach at the same time. Our time is five-thirty on Thursday night."

"That's smart," Deanna said. "That'll have us going in during dinner. Crews have either left or are on dinner break. If that's the case, then we just need to figure out how to get into the facility."

"That's going to be the tricky part," Eddie agreed.

"Good thing we have some time to figure it out," Wyatt said.

"I just hope it's enough time," Eddie said. "I have a feeling he's just waiting for us."

Wyatt countered, "Then you had better be ready."

PAYBACK TIME

"People often complain about lack of time when lack of direction is the real problem." Zig Ziglar

"Do you think she'll be okay?" Gemma asked Bells as they sat in Hope's room.

"I hope so," Bells said. "I'm not sure how that will affect Wyatt if she dies. He was torn about leaving in the first place. If she dies while he's gone, he may never forgive himself."

Gemma turned back to Hope and gave her hand a gentle squeeze. "I know you don't know us, but we know your kids and Wyatt. We cannot wait to meet you."

"I could tap into some of her memories to give her good ones to hold onto?" Bells offered.

"I think that's a great idea," Gemma said. "Go ahead. I'll keep watch."

Bells went to the opposite side of the bed from Gemma and sat down in a chair. When she took Hope's hand into hers,

Gemma let it go so she would not get pulled into the memories. Bells closed her eyes and took a deep, cleansing breath…

◁◁◁▷▷

WALKING in a space void of color or sound, she saw Hope sitting in a chair by herself. Hope had her arms wrapped around her legs as she rocked in the chair. Tears streaked her face.

"Hope?" Bells asked.

"Who are you?" Hope furrowed her brow. "Where am I? How did I get here?"

Crouching in front of her, Bells gently touched Hope's knee as she calmly explained, "Hope, my name is Isabelle."

"As in Isabelle from Maine?"

"Yes. My gift allows me to go into a person's mind. I can also control emotions and read minds. I'm not as good at it as Adam or Blake, but I can do it. There are some things I need to talk to you about, and then I want you to show me some things."

"What's going on?"

"You remember when Blake and Deanna pulled you out of the dungeon?" Bells asked.

"Yes."

"When they pulled you, you were very sick."

"I know. They poisoned me. Am I dead? I feel like I'm dead."

"No. The hospital is doing its best to get the poison out of your system while also focusing on getting you back to good nutritional health."

"I see. Where are the others?"

"We're all safe for now, and so are you. Gemma and I are watching over you. Mac, Shawn, Lindsey, Tanya, and Megan are at a hotel near us."

"Why are they here?" Hope asked, horrified. "They're not supposed to be here! What happened?"

"Please stay calm. I'm doing my best to keep us both calm, but going into someone's mind takes a lot out of me."

"Okay. I'm sorry."

"Don't worry about it. I just need you to stay calm. If you spiral, there's no telling where we could end up. Coming into this void is actually a good thing. That tells me that you locked yourself away to reserve your strength."

"Why are the teens here?" Hope asked again.

"The Professor found out they know about the Clinic. He doesn't know how much, but he was going to kidnap them to find out. They got out before that happened to make sure their families were safe."

"I see. And the others?"

"Right now, Wyatt's driving Deanna, Freya, and Eddie to Oregon to rescue more of our brothers and sisters, while Colby is driving Holly, Blake, and Adam to Wyoming to get the others."

"I see. And, Ben?"

"We'll get to him in a moment. I want you to be in a good headspace when we talk about his condition. In the meantime, we're going in the direction of good memories. Can you take me on some of those?"

"I can do that," Hope said. She put her feet down and shifted so Bells could comfortably sit on the arm of the chair. Together, they watched the memories play around them as if they were in a surround movie experience. Only the characters in the memory ignored their presence…

ORANGE, yellow, and red streaks flashed all around them. Giggling children could be heard as the streaks started to come into focus. It was a beautiful autumn day. Bells could smell the hay from the hay maze. She could feel the sun on her face as they sat on the chair.

"This was one of the Sunday outings. The kids absolutely loved fall. With their birthday at the beginning of October, it was always a time of celebration," Hope explained quietly, so as not to interrupt the scene. "The kids were about three at the time."

Just then, three-year-old Holly came running out of the maze, being chased by three-year-old Blake. They were laughing and giggling as they played catch. Ben and Hope each had a pumpkin.

"The kids picked their pumpkins before the maze," Hope said. "We learned that year to wait until after the maze. The size pumpkins they picked always seemed massive. They weighed at least five to ten pounds each."

"That sounds heavy. I've never seen a real pumpkin," Bells admitted.

Hope looked up at her, astounded. "Really?"

"Nope."

"So, you never made pumpkin seeds, pumpkin muffins, or carved a pumpkin?"

"No."

"Wow," Hope said and let out a low whistle. "We have a lot to catch y'all up on!"

"And, we'll enjoy each experience together," Bells encouraged, giving Hope's shoulder a gentle squeeze.

Turning back toward the memory, they watched as a nice couple took some photos with Hope's phone while the family sat on a rock.

"They're adorable," Bells said, hoping to keep Hope focused on the good and give her a reason to fight.

"They were," Hope agreed. "Holly always had these adorable pig-tails, and Blake's hair was always covering his eyes. But we always got compliments about how cute and well-behaved they were."

"They were adorable, and are striking teens," Bells agreed.

After they left the field, the next memory was of the family at home on that same day, carving out the pumpkin. Bells inhaled deeply at the smell of the pumpkin muffins cooking.

"That smells divine!" Bells said. "I cannot imagine what they taste like."

Hope gently tapped Bells' leg. "We'll get there."

"I hope so!"

They continued to watch as Wyatt arrived, and the tiny family made pumpkin seeds in the oven. While the seeds were cooking, they paired up, so Blake and Ben did one pumpkin, and Wyatt and Holly carved the other pumpkin, with Hope as the judge.

Ben and Blake made an intricate design that looked like a battle between space ships in space. Meanwhile, Wyatt and Holly made a crazy design of different flowers and butterflies.

Hope carefully studied both pumpkins. Shaking her head, she declared, "Tie! They are both amazing! Great job!"

The teams gave each other high-fives as the scene faded to black.

"Was that a normal October?" Bells asked.

"Actually, it was. We often took Sunday outings as a family. When we got home, Wyatt would come over, and we would just hang as a family. We're a unique blend, but it worked for us."

"I have to admit I'm jealous of the way Blake and Holly were raised."

"That's okay, honey. You'll get there when we get back to Texas."

"Wyatt promised to find us all homes."

"Don't doubt him at his word. If he promised you, it will get done. Here's another good one," Hope said and turned her attention to the swirling blue, gray, and green.

As the memory came into focus, Hope and Bells were sitting on the chair in the middle of the woods. Hearing sirens blaring in the distance, they turned to see Holly, Blake, Ben, and Hope running through the woods toward the house.

"Are we going to make it?" ten-year-old Holly asked.

Hearing the sound of a roar that resembled a train, Blake shouted, "It's close!"

Holly stopped short. When the others realized she stopped running, they turned to see what she was doing.

Holly saw the funnel cloud in the distance. She thrust her hands forward. Straining herself, she nudged the funnel cloud so it circumvented the home. The debris cloud moved closer to them, but Holly ran up to the trio and pushed her hands forward. Any debris that came near them split off to the right or left of the group.

"You got this, sis!" Blake encouraged, while Ben held Hope, fear written all over them.

Holly stood her ground for several minutes before the funnel cloud moved on. While there was damage to the house and workshop, it was nowhere near what it should have been with the F3 tornado.

"That was a scary day," Hope said, watching the family walk back home, with Ben carrying Holly. "We didn't like to push them to the point of exhaustion. Holly did that on her own. I didn't like it when she did it, but she always was a stubborn one. You couldn't tell her what to do."

Bells snickered. "I can only imagine."

While they sat there, the image faded to black before another swirl of white, light orange, black, and blue mixed all around them. Bells smelled the scents of popcorn and funnel cakes. She could hear the yelling, screaming, and delight of a party. The swirling gave way to a vision unlike anything Bells had ever seen before. "What is this place?" Bells stood, looking around in awe.

The Ferris wheel spun. The various stands had people playing games. There were multiple rides, including one that swung in the air while people rode in swings. It was night, but the streets were lit up with the lights.

"It's a fair. It comes to town every year. The kids were fourteen at the time. Blake and Holly loved all the rides and games. Holly's favorites were the funnel cakes and the ride where the floor dropped. Blake devoured cotton candy and popcorn, and his favorite ride was the swings. He said it gave him space, and when it was in the air, he could see for a good distance, yet keep an eye on the people around them," Hope explained.

"I could see that." Bells nodded. "So, when we get to Texas, is this something we can go to as well?"

"Definitely!"

Hope and Bells looked on as the tiny family of four made their way through the maze of people to the various rides. After one ride on the Ferris wheel, Blake seemed really upset.

"What's wrong?" Ben asked. "You look angry."

"The boy in the cart behind Holly and I thought some not-nice thoughts about Holly," Blake admitted. "I tried to block it, but I couldn't. I can't tell Holly either, even though she should know."

"Go ahead," Hope said to Ben, eavesdropping on their conversation. She still listened while she and Holly got in line for a funnel cake.

Resting his arm over Blake's shoulder, the pair sat down on a bench. "Son, it's like this. You're at an age where hormones will rule your thoughts," Ben explained.

"I don't have those thoughts about other girls. I may think they're pretty or want to kiss them, but definitely not what that kid thought! I don't even know where to start with the ugly things that went through his mind."

"No need. I was a young kid once. All your mom and I ask is that you and Holly respect the opposite sex. We know hormones will soon take over, and we'll do our best to guide and direct you, but ultimately how it looks is up to you. Just understand many choices you make will affect you for the rest of your life."

"I'm not sure what you mean by that."

"That may be more of a conversation you and I have together when we're not in the middle of a fair," Ben said with a wink.

"What's going on?" Holly asked, snacking on her funnel cake.

Hope handed Blake cotton candy and a drink.

"There was a guy who didn't think kind things about you," Blake said before Ben or Hope could stop him.

"Who was it?" Holly asked.

"See that kid in the red shirt with those other boys?" Blake pointed them out.

"Okay. I think we need to move on," Ben said, sensing Holly's temper start to flare.

"I'm not stopping her," Blake said. "She needs to defend herself."

The boy looked up at Holly. He smiled and winked at her.

When Holly saw that, she narrowed her eyes at him. "How dare he!" she said in a low growl.

Suddenly the guy in the dunk tank the guys were standing next to dropped into the tank. No one was even in line to throw at the target, so it took everyone by surprise. The corndogs, funnel cakes, cotton candy, popcorn, fried cakes, and drinks the boys were holding were all coated with the chlorinated water of the dunk tank when the water splashed over. Holly gave her hand a swipe, creating a bigger wave from the dunk tank, coating all the boys in water.

The boys started yelling at the dunk tank operator about their food, clothes, and how their phones got soaked, completely forgetting about Holly.

"Serves them right," Holly said with a satisfied smile.

"Doesn't serve the dunk tank operator right," Hope pointed out. "He suffered for your revenge."

Holly's elated moment sunk. She dropped her head in shame.

"Maybe you should take a couple drinks and a funnel cake over to the operator and the dunk tank person as an apology for the rudeness of the boys toward them…using your own money?" Hope suggested.

"Yes, ma'am," Holly said, handing her mom her cake to hold while she did what her mom suggested.

"I was actually quite proud of her that day," Hope said to Bells. "While I get the negative outcome, she stood up for herself. Then, she also made up for her error in judgment. She learned to control her actions. Had she left it to just the original splash, the damage to the phones of the boys wouldn't have happened, and they wouldn't have been so irate."

"I see," Bells said in understanding. "So, many of these memories seem to contain a lot of guidance."

"They do. That's my job as their mother. As parents, we guide and direct in love."

"I wouldn't know anything about that," Bells pointed out.

Tapping Bells' hand, Hope encouraged, "You will soon. On to the next memory."

The room swirled in blue, white, red, and green around them until they were in a strawberry field, picking strawberries.

"The kids were only thirteen here," Hope explained. "We paid for the strawberries by weight. I'm so glad we didn't have to put the kids on the scale!" Hope chuckled. "They would eat one or two and put one in the basket. They basically ate their way through the field."

"So, you can just go to farms and pick their strawberries?" Bells asked, amazed.

"You have to pay for it, and not all farms allow you to do it, but yes, some do."

They watched for several minutes before the memory shifted to inside the kitchen at the house. Blake and Ben cleaned the strawberries in the sink, while Holly and Hope ripped the tops off of the strawberries and then places them in a colander to continue to dry off.

Blake glanced at Ben out of the corner of his eyes, with a sly smile on his face.

"Oh no," Bells said, dropping her head into her hand, shaking it.

"Oh yes," Hope said, laughing.

Blake took a second and then splashed the water toward Ben.

"Hey!" Ben objected. Then he splashed water on Blake. Blake grabbed the sprayer of the sink while Ben continued to use the water from the spigot. Meanwhile, Holly and Hope just did their best to stay out of the water.

The water fight went on for a few minutes before Holly decided to end it. She raised two giant handfuls of strawberries into the air over their heads. Both guys stopped and looked up. When they did, she slammed the strawberries into their faces.

"Oh geez!" Bells laughed. "Guess Holly got the last word in."

Hope shook her head. "Guess again!"

Both Ben and Blake looked at each other for only a moment before Blake turned the sprayer on Holly and Hope. Ben ran around the counter and wrapped his arms around both of them, holding them in place while Blake continued to soak them with the sprayer.

The scene faded as everyone was laughing and having a good time.

Hope and Bells sat in the black room, still on the chair.

"Good memories," Hope said. "Ones I will treasure forever, whether here on earth or in Heaven."

"What do you mean?" Bells asked.

"That's right!" Hope face-palmed herself. "You wouldn't be exposed to Christ in the facility."

"No. I have caught bits and pieces, though. And, I know you said Ben accepted Christ. That's why Blake didn't want the memory taken from you."

"Memory taken from me? Can you do that?" Hope asked.

"We can. It's tricky until you know what you're doing. It takes a lot out of you, but it is possible."

"No. I know what I experienced in the clinic was rough, but to know Ben is now in Heaven and at peace brings me happiness."

"I don't understand."

"Let's let a memory fill in part of it," Hope said, as swirls of burnt orange, a dark gray metal color, and white light whipped around them until the room Hope was secured in became clear.

"I think I'm going to be sick," Bells said in a groan.

"It's okay. As you can see, it's my memory, not yours."

"Hope!" Ben called out.

"I'm here, Ben! I didn't know if you were still with me," Hope called back as she was zip-tied to the chair.

"I am. I need to tell you what happened that day."

"With Joey?" Hope asked.

"Yes."

"I'm listening," she said. As long as she heard his voice, she knew he was still with her.

"We were coming home for a break. Mom, Dad, Noah, Eve, and Abigail were at a pageant at church," he said and coughed up more blood. After he spit to clear his mouth, he continued, "We pulled into the house around five-thirty. They were due home shortly. I got out of the car, and a shot rang out. I felt it pierce my leg as I dropped to the ground. Joey ran around to help me. When she did, her father ran out from behind a bush. She looked up, too stunned to say anything. Before she could run, he shot her in the chest. She immediately dropped to the ground, but to me, everything happened in slow motion. I grabbed her as her dad ran away, holding her to my chest. She was my sister, despite not being born into the family. We were as close as siblings born in the same family. Joey had a look of peace on her face. Her body was riddled with pain, but she still looked serene. She told me to use her death to lead others to Christ. And then, she closed her eyes. My family pulled in, with the police not too far behind. A neighbor called the police and an ambulance. She was already gone. As she left, my heart hardened."

"I'm so sorry, Ben."

"I was furious with God. There were people who came to Christ through her story, but I was angry. I turned my back on God. I left Bible college. Instead, I went to a community college and became a nurse. My relationship with Jesus was never the same. I wanted nothing to do with Him."

"He still never left you," Hope encouraged.

"I left Him and never looked back…until now. I don't want to come back just because I'm dying."

"You're not dying."

"Yes, Hope! I am dying. We're medical. We know what death looks like. There is blood all over my clothes. I've seen the pictures of those women. I've seen death before, Hope. I don't have much time. My life's been playing through my mind. I'm going to die…soon."

"Ben, my heart hurts for you. I don't know what to do."

"As you said, it's not my job, nor your job to save me. Only Christ can do that."

"He did. You said you were one of His," Hope said.

"I want to be one of His again. Will you pray with me, Hope?"

"Yes."

"God," Ben said, looking toward Heaven, "I know I haven't been the best witness for you in this life. I know I've done wrong. I ask You to accept me back into your family. I know I don't deserve it, but I ask for Your grace and mercy. I miss You. Jesus, I know I turned my back on You. I know You did nothing to deserve it. I know it was from the evil in this world. I ask You to forgive me for all I've done. I ask You to be with me at this moment. I know I won't be in this body for much longer, and ask that when I do pass on, I'll be in Your presence? Please forgive me? Please allow me back into your family? I'm sorry," Ben said, tears crawling down his cheeks.

"He heard you, Ben. Matthew 18:20 promises, *'For where two or three are gathered together in My name, there am I in the midst of them.'* He's here, Ben. He's here. He's been waiting for you to come home again."

"Home," Ben said with a smile.

A form of a Man wearing white, with a bright light glowing around Him, suddenly appeared before Ben. As He spread His arms toward Ben, Ben saw the nail prints in His hands.

"He's here," Ben said.

"Who's here?" Hope asked, heart racing, thinking it was Professor Roth.

"Thank you for forgiving me," Ben said. "I commend my soul and spirit to you today."

With that, his breath left his body, and his head dropped.

Hope closed her eyes. Seeing all of this in her mind allowed her to be with Ben in his last moments. "Welcome home, Ben. I'll be there to give you a hug when it's my time. I love you, brother. Take care of him, Lord. He's yours now. The prodigal son has returned just in time."

As Hope looked toward the ceiling, tears running down her cheeks, the room started to swirl together again.

"Wow," Bells said, wiping the tears from her eyes. "That was beautiful."

"That's why Blake didn't want you to take the memory from me."

"Who was that man with Ben in the end?"

"Per the nail prints in His hands, I'm sure it was Jesus Himself. I know Ben is currently in Heaven looking down on us right now, thanks to the vision God granted me."

"I understand and feel the emotions behind this. What I don't understand is this Jesus," Bells admitted as they sat again in the dark room.

Looking up, Hope prayed for the right words. "Deanna, Adam, Blake, Holly, and Wyatt all came to the facility to rescue all y'all. Right?"

"Right."

"That took a lot of faith in trust in each other to pull it off. It also could have resulted in one or all of them losing their lives."

"But they didn't."

"They didn't know that would be the result," Hope pointed out.

"And, just like Maine, they're now taking their lives into their own hands to rescue the others," Bells said in understanding.

"Exactly. Any or all could lose their lives. We may never see any of them again. Knowing that fact, they chose to go anyway."

"I see."

"Just like they're willing to give up their lives for each other, there is One who came and did give up His life for everyone. He knew He was coming to die. And the cool thing? Even if it was only for you, He still would have done it!"

"Why?"

"Let me see how to put this." Hope tapped her chin in thought. "Even though you don't know Him, Jesus knew you before you were even in the womb. He created you. He loves you more than you know."

"Created me? Like Professor Roth?"

"No. Not like Professor Roth. Professor Roth didn't create you. He manipulated your genes and was part of the process of your birth, but he did not create you. God did. And, God doesn't make mistakes."

"Okay," Bells said, following along.

"A long time ago, Adam and Eve were created by God. Adam and Eve messed up, though. They were given everything they could ever want, with only one rule. That rule was they were not allowed to eat of the fruit of the Tree of Knowledge."

"That sounds like a set-up."

"It wasn't a set-up. He wanted them to obey. He wanted them to be happy and satisfied with God and all He gave them. However, they were tempted by Satan, who was represented by the snake. He tempted them, and they failed. In that instant, sin entered the world. Now, back in those days, when someone sinned, they had to offer a sacrifice to make up for it. This sacrifice had to be a perfect animal. In other words, the best animal in the flock."

"Why?"

"Because there had to be a penalty for sin. There had to be blood shed from a perfect sacrifice. Well, long story short, after thousands of years, God and Jesus got together. They had an idea. Instead of everyone sacrificing animals, there could be an ultimate sacrifice. This sacrifice had to cost everything, and it had to be from One who was perfect. It had to also be a blood sacrifice."

"But Who is Jesus and Who is God?" Bells asked.

"God is the creator of the world. He is so powerful, He only had to speak the world into existence."

"Wow!"

"Exactly! Do you know what angels are?"

"No."

"Angels are those who God created to serve Him in Heaven. God is the ultimate power. His angels have quite a bit of power. Lucifer used to be one of his top angels. While God was creating the world, Lucifer took the opportunity to try to take over Heaven. He even convinced some other angels to join him."

"Uh-oh!"

"Yeah. That didn't go well. When God found out, he kicked Lucifer and his followers out of Heaven. Remember that snake?"

"Yeah."

"Remember how I said that was Satan in the form of a snake?"

"Yes."

"Satan and Lucifer are the same entity."

"Oh! So, if I'm following you, Satan tried to overtake Heaven. When that didn't work, God kicked him out of Heaven down to Earth."

"Yes."

"And, after God made Adam and Eve, Satan, also Lucifer, tried to get Adam and Eve on his side by getting them to break the rule?"

"Yes! Good job! That's a really hard concept to understand. Well done!"

"Thank you!"

"Now, as I said, thousands of years passed. Jesus, Who is the Son of God, and God, Who is The Father, the Creator of the world and everything in it, were talking. They figured out a plan in order to help those who were on Earth. If Jesus came to Earth and gave His life, shedding His blood, then those who believed in Him and follow Him would be able to live in eternity with Jesus and God."

"What happens if they don't follow or believe in this Jesus?" Bells asked.

"Well, the alternative to Heaven is Hell. Satan and his followers know that is their eternal punishment. They do their best to make sure more join them in this punishment."

"What is Hell?"

"Heaven has lakes of crystal, streets of gold, and a Throne Room where God resides next to none! There are no more tears or pain...ever...for eternity. On the flip-side, there's Hell. Hell is a lake of fire. It smells like smoke and brimstone. There will be wailing and gnashing of teeth. There will be eternal torment."

"I would think that would be an easy choice."

"Here's the thing," Hope continued. "When Adam and Eve broke that rule, it initially cut us off from God. The only way to gain forgiveness for our sin was to make the sacrifice we talked about earlier."

"Right."

"That moment when they broke the rule, eternity changed for all of humanity."

"How?"

"Before that rule was broken, we would have automatically gone to Heaven to be with God when we died. Now, because that rule was broken, we are automatically going to Hell once we reach an age of understanding, unless we choose to follow Jesus and go to Heaven when we die."

"But I thought Jesus made the sacrifice you talked about? Wouldn't that change things?"

"Oh! It did. It gave us a choice. We don't have to go to Hell. We can make a choice to follow Jesus and go to Heaven, just like Ben did. When Jesus was crucified on the cross, He died. They buried Him."

"That was the sacrifice, right?"

"Right," Hope said, pleased she was following along. "Now, He didn't stay dead. On the third day, He rose from the grave. He's alive!"

"Alive? As in flesh and blood like we are? Now, that's some gift!"

"Jesus is not like you. He is the Son of The Lord God! He's stronger than any human would or could be, no matter what's done to their DNA. Jesus didn't have to give His life for humanity – He chose to. He chose to come down from Heaven. He chose to live amongst humanity, so you would know He understands you. He chose to let those coming after Him take Him, even though He knew what they were going to do. He chose to stay, despite them whipping His back with a cruel instrument called a cat-o'-nine-tails. He chose to let them hang Him on a cross. He chose to go through with the sacrifice, despite the pain and agony, for you, for your eternal security. He loved you before you were formed in your mother's womb, and He still loved you today. He wants you to choose Him."

◁◁◁▷▷

"You called for us?" Officer Shultz asked. He was the chief of security at the Oregon facility. He and the supervisors from all the shifts walked into The Professor's office. "I apologize for the delay. Many had to come from home. However, you said it was an emergency."

"It is," The Professor said, looking up from his work. Setting his pen down, he interlaced his fingers in front of him and stated, "Ladies and gentlemen, we have a problem. I've learned throughout the years to not waste time. There is a storm heading our way."

"What do you mean?" Officer Shultz asked.

"The Maine facility was targeted a few days ago, and the subjects were stolen."

"What?" Officer Shultz's jaw dropped. "How is that possible?"

"We were overrun," The Professor explained. "I do not want the same thing to happen here. "The subjects must be protected at all costs."

"Sir?"

"At all costs, Officer. You have your orders. Lock this place down until further notice. No one in or out."

"Sir, that's not proper procedure. You put the procedures in place, so everything was run to your design. The only reason to lock the facility down that tightly is if there is an imminent threat on the campus."

Professor Roth narrowed his eyes. "Are you arguing with me on how to protect my facility?"

"I'm not one to argue, sir. I just don't want to get into trouble by doing something against orders and then paying for it later.

Besides, these people have families at home they have to get back to. For example, Evelyn here has children at the sitter. She's a single mom. She can't afford to be in forever lockdown. A lockdown normally doesn't last more than several hours at most. You're talking about a lockdown without even a target date to lift the lock. I'm sorry, but I cannot do that."

"Is this true, Evelyn?" Professor Roth asked her.

"It is true that I am a single mother, and my children are at the sitter when I am here at work," Evelyn confirmed.

"You may be dismissed with pay until the lockdown is complete," Professor Roth told her. Turning back to Officer Shultz, he said, "See? I'm not without a heart."

"Sir, there are more in that type of situation," Officer Shultz argued.

Professor Roth braced his hands on the desk in front of him as he stood, almost seeming to double in size. Intimidating was a kind word for it. "Officer Shultz, here is what I need you to do. Call in officers who can do this indefinitely. Supervisors like Evelyn here are the only ones excused with pay. If they have a spouse or are living with a family who can care for the children, they are not excused. If they leave or do not show up, then they can find another job. Do I make myself clear?"

"Y-yes, s-sir," Officer Shultz stammered. "Consider it done."

"Thank you. You are dismissed."

"Thank you, sir," Officer Shultz said, and he and the others left.

After the supervisors cleared his office, Professor Roth hit the intercom to his secretary. Her voice crackled over the speaker, "Yes, sir?"

"Get my daughter on the phone immediately. She is at the Wyoming Facility."

"Yes, sir," she said, and the line went dead.

"How dare he argue with me regarding my own facility!"

Professor Roth crossed his arms as he dropped into his chair. "The nerve!"

His intercom beeped. His secretary said, "Sir, Alex is on the line."

"Put her through."

"Yes, sir. Alex, go ahead," she said and dropped her line.

"Hey, Daddy," Alex's voice came through the speakerphone.

Professor Roth stood and paced his office. "Alex, I need you to lock down the Wyoming Facility."

"For how long?"

"Indefinitely."

"Daddy, I can't do –"

"Why do people persist in arguing with me over this?" he snapped, cutting her off. "Find those who can, and fire the rest. Understood?"

"Yes, sir."

"We don't know which one they will hit first. We need to be ready. Once one is hit, call the other to warn them."

"Yes, sir."

"If they come here first, you'll have fifteen hours to fortify the facility. Same for me if they hit you first."

"What will you do if they hit them at the same time?" Alex asked.

"They don't have the manpower to do that," The Professor dismissed her. "Just be ready. Lock it down. Understood?"

"Yes, sir," Alex said and hung up.

"Time to buckle down," The Professor said, slamming his hands on his desk. As he crumpled the papers under his hands, he glared at no one in particular, as he growled, "No one takes anything away from me and lives to tell about it. They caught me off-guard once. Their time of freedom is up. They are now out of time!"

With the Maine Facility teens released and the Willow Bend teens safely tucked away, the next phase was to rescue the kids from the Wyoming and Oregon Facilities.

Colby is driving Holly, Blake, and Adam to the Wyoming Facility. Meanwhile, Wyatt is driving Deanna, Eddie, and Freya to the Oregon facility. Both teams are unaware The Professor is waiting for them with plans in place.With both facilities in lockdown, will the teens be able to rescue their siblings? Will Hope pull through from the damage inflicted by Professor Roth? Are the Willow Bend teens, Gemma, Bells, and Hope safe all the way over in Philadelphia, or are they still a target? Everyone has to be ready for this mental chess game. Moves and countermoves are being made. Calculations are continuously changing. Who will come out the victor? Will it be The Professor or the teens? Can the teens succeed, or are they ***Out Of Time***?

. . .

1 Peter 5:8 – "Be sober, be vigilant; because your adversary the devil, as a roaring lion, walketh about, seeking whom he may devour."

Jeremiah 29:11 – "For I know the plans I have for you," declares the Lord, "plans to prosper you and not to harm you, plans to give you hope and a future.

"Time slips through our hands like grains of sand never to return again. Those who use time wisely are rewarded with rich, productive and satisfying lives." Robin Sharma

BOOKS BY C.J. PETERSON

**Grace Restored Series can be found: https://cjpetersonwrites.com/
series-books**

**Holy Flame Trilogy can be found: https://cjpetersonwrites.com/
series-books**

**Divine Legacy Series can be found: https://cjpetersonwrites.com/
series-books**

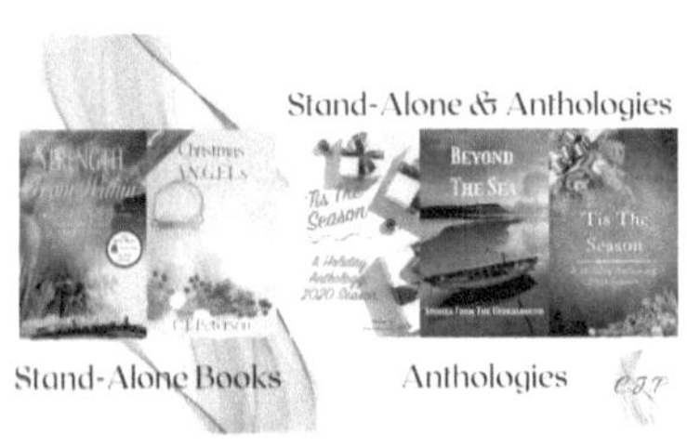

C.J.'s Stand-Alone Books & Anthologies She Participated in can be found:

https://cjpetersonwrites.com/stand-alone-%26-anthologies

'Tis The Season, A Holiday Anthology: 2021 Season to be released OCT2021

Sands of Time Trilogy can be found: https://cjpetersonwrites.com/series-books

Out of Time to be released JAN2022